The FLiP FLOP Club

Charmed Summer

Coming soon in The Flip-Flop Club series:

Whale Song
Midnight Messages
Star Struck

Charmed Summer

Ellen Richardson

Series created by Working Partners Ltd

OXFORD
UNIVERSITY PRESS

OXFORD
UNIVERSITY PRESS

Great Clarendon Street, Oxford OX2 6DP

Oxford University Press is a department of the University of Oxford.
It furthers the University's objective of excellence in research, scholarship,
and education by publishing worldwide in

Oxford   New York

Auckland   Cape Town   Dar es Salaam   Hong Kong   Karachi
Kuala Lumpur   Madrid   Melbourne   Mexico City   Nairobi
New Delhi   Shanghai   Taipei   Toronto

With offices in

Argentina   Austria   Brazil   Chile   Czech Republic   France   Greece
Guatemala   Hungary   Italy   Japan   Poland   Portugal   Singapore
South Korea   Switzerland   Thailand   Turkey   Ukraine   Vietnam

Oxford is a registered trade mark of Oxford University Press
in the UK and in certain other countries

British Library Cataloguing in Publication Data
Data available

ISBN: 978-0-19-275661-9
1 3 5 7 9 10 8 6 4 2

Printed in Great Britain

Paper used in the production of this book is a natural,
recyclable product made from wood grown in sustainable forests.
The manufacturing process conforms to the environmental
regulations of the country of origin.

For Lydia

I enjoyed this book very much, everyone should read it!
Catherine, *age 12*

What's going to happen next? I can't wait!
Fan-tabby-dashes!
Lauren, *age 9*

Be prepared to experience heartbreak, happiness
and hilariousness in this awesome book!
Alice, *age 10*

I would definitely recommend it to my mates!
Mollie, *age 13*

Mojo the dog is really cute!
Amy, *age 9*

I felt like I was there with the girls . . . my least favourite
thing about the book was that it came to an end!
Ellie, *age 8 $\frac{3}{4}$*

Three best friends making mischief – I love it!
Molly, *age 9*

Mystery, good adventures, and a few scary bits!
A good book to read on a cold, rainy day!
Tabitha, *age 8*

I don't really like reading books, but I loved reading
Charmed Summer! I think that it's the best book that I
have ever read.
Emily, *age 12*

I couldn't put it down!!
Amelia, *age 9*

A very original, colourful, cheerful and rather
intriguing story. I would really love to read the next
book, and when they come out I will probably
buy the whole series.
Amneet, *age 10 $^1/_3$*

A summer full of magic and fun . . . you
should definitely read this book!
Lily, *age 9*

Sierra's my favourite character because she's like me!
Emily, *age 10*

A very dramatic book!
Sierra is my Favourite
Anna 6

Chapter 1

She wasn't going to make it! Waves were already breaking over the causeway as Elly sprinted past the milestone marking the halfway point. She splashed through foam, soaking her trainers. It was taking longer than she had expected to run to the mainland and back. But she had to do something. She loved Aunt Dina, but if she had to crochet one more tea cosy she was going to scream.

She pumped her legs faster. Soon the only way on or off Sunday Island would disappear under the sea. As she raced the tide, Elly remembered one of her mum's acting jobs

from years ago—the one where a monster wave destroyed a seaside town. Mum had been eighth in the credits, her best ever. Elly tried to pretend this was a film set and she was the star shooting the big action sequence. But her heart gave a little hiccup as she noticed the sea was swallowing the causeway faster than she could run. All thoughts of *lights, camera, action* vanished. Elly picked up speed.

The waves were over her feet now. A few butterflies—giant mutant moths, actually—started flapping around her insides as she watched the last of the causeway disappear. Only the fence and a row of flags marked the road.

Don't freak! Nothing bad would happen. But she knew all too well that happy endings were only guaranteed in PG. Life was 12+.

A horn sounded behind her and she stumbled to one side as a rusty Ford Focus surged past, drenching her with spray. The driver called out of the window. 'Get off the causeway! It's dangerous!'

'Hey, wait!' Elly stared after him.

Even in those few seconds the tide had risen. It was up to her knees now. Her feet were frozen and she was gasping for air like a stranded fish. She glanced at the island. The tall, windswept hill that islanders jokingly called 'The Mountain' rose from the centre of Sunday Island. The town crouched at its feet. She could even see Aunt Dina's cottage tucked into the slope of the hill. Ten minutes walk from here. Dead easy . . . if it weren't for the sea trying to kill her.

She sloshed forward, slipped, fell and got a mouthful of salt water. Elly scrabbled to her feet. A sob broke through her gasping breaths.

She couldn't die like this and leave Dad all alone. She shoved fear away and kept moving.

The whine of a motor boat made her jerk her head towards the sound. She balanced against the pull and push of the sea and windmilled her arms frantically. The woman driving gave Elly a cheerful wave as the motorboat did a U-turn at full throttle and sped back to open water.

Panic returned at the sight of the boat's wake rushing towards her. It crashed across the causeway and swept over her, knocking her down, closing over her head. She was in the water, tumbling across concrete, scraping elbows, knees, hands. She was choking, too breathless to scream as the sea dragged her towards deep water. She was going to drown.

It would kill Dad. She remembered his face,

in those horrible days after Mum's funeral. He wouldn't survive another loss.

The water slammed her into something hard. Coughing and spluttering, she hauled herself upright and found she was clinging to the fence that ran along one side of the causeway. The sea was waist-deep now, the tide still coming in. Her heart was thudding with hope as well as fear now. Holding tight to the railing, Elly pulled herself through the water to the nearest fence post and scrambled up until she was balanced above the waves on its circular top.

The beach was less than fifty metres away. Her feet were still numb, but the top rail of the fence looked sturdy. She took a deep breath and began to inch along it. The waves were getting bigger. One crashed against the fence, shooting spray waist-high. Elly wobbled but kept moving.

Closer . . . Closer . . . And, at last, she was there! Standing on the warm glittering sand of Sunday Island.

Her legs went limp as rubber bands. She plopped onto the sand and lay on her back, watching the sky spin past. That had been totally amazing.

'*What in the name of Venus, Mars and milkshakes did you think you were doing?*'

Elly lurched upright. Aunt Dina marched across the sand, her cloud of black hair, silk scarves and tinkling jewellery bouncing with each stride. Before Elly could say a word, her aunt wrapped her in a bear hug. 'Are you trying to get yourself killed?' Aunt Dina's voice boomed through layers of silk and squishiness. 'Did you even think what that would do to Nick? Or me?' There was a loud sniff.

Being hugged by Aunt Dina was like being cuddled by

a walking duvet. She smelt of vanilla and finger paints—Mum's smell. Suddenly Elly's eyes pricked with tears. She blinked them away and gave her aunt a quick kiss. 'I'm Super-Elly, remember? I jump over flooded causeways in a single bound!' It was a joke from the old days, when her aunt had lived with them while going to art school in London. Before Gran died and Aunt Dina moved into the cottage on Sunday Island. Before Mum's cancer.

Her aunt laughed but shook her head. 'You can't get out of it that easy, El.'

'You won't tell Dad, will you?'

'I ought to.' Aunt Dina frowned down at her, one eyebrow raised. 'But Nick's had enough grief. And we don't want him worried—he might take you back to London. You'd be shut up in that stuffy flat all day on your own. I won't tell him. But you scare me like this

again and just you see what happens! For now, you are *so* grounded.'

Elly kicked the sand into puffs as she followed her aunt up the beach. Her shorts and T–shirt were already drying in the sun. 'How did you know where to find me?'

'Mr Portas phoned and said he'd driven past a crazy girl on the causeway and did I know where my niece was.'

Elly hated this stupid island. She'd rather be back in London—at least she'd have her friends, even if they did treat her differently now that she was the girl with the dead mum. Her aunt marched on, head erect, eyes forward.

They passed through the hillocks of marram grass lining the beach and emerged onto the main road. Elly had to trot to keep up as Aunt Dina surged up the high street. She 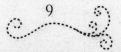 was painfully aware of other islanders calling greetings to her aunt, who waved back while continuing to lecture in her megaphone voice.

'Disappearing for hours on end without a word to tell me where you've gone or when you'll be back. After today I dread to think what other hare-brained things you might get up to. Your best jeans ripped to shreds yesterday. Just how did you do that?'

While trying to keep from being bored to death. Elly remembered her attempt at sandboarding yesterday, using a bit of planking she'd found behind the garden shed, and winced. She opened her mouth to explain.

'No!' said Aunt Dina. 'Don't tell me. I don't want to know!'

She hadn't finished her lecture. Up the hill and onto the lane, every word blaring, tourists turning to stare. By the time they reached the cottage, Elly was so full of shiny embarrassment she thought she would burst.

She scrambled up the attic ladder into her bedroom and immediately felt better. She loved this room. It had sloping walls plastered between roof beams and two dormer windows, one looking out to sea, one facing the big hill. Its crazy, tilting wooden floor was scattered with handmade rugs that matched the patchwork quilt on the small brass bed. Best of all, it had been her mother's bedroom when she was young.

Elly went to the dresser and picked up the silver-framed photo she had brought with her from home. It was a photo of her and her mum on the set of *London Pride*, the soap that had made Mum semi-famous for a few years. When she got pregnant in real life, they had written a baby into the script. Elly

had been on and off
the screen from the
time she was a bump
till she was nearly two.
Shame she couldn't remember
any of it.

She glanced in the mirror. Her skin was a lighter brown, but she had her mother's thick, curly black hair. And even if she had inherited Dad's nose, at least she had Mum's mouth and her love for movies. Her mother had said Elly was a good actor. But that was the sort of thing mums say. Elly sighed and replaced the photograph.

How was she going to get through this summer? She had been exiled to Sunday Island as soon as school had finished. Did Dad expect her to spend the whole summer without friends? Or TV? Aunt Dina thought TV rotted your brain. The island didn't even have a cinema. There was only one internet café and that was shut half the time.

She plopped down at the desk nestling in the seaward dormer and fished her mobile out of the drawer. Dad *had* to let her come home. She punched in his number but nothing happened. No signal again. Sunday-Rubbish-Island had bad mobile reception on top of everything else.

Elly dropped the phone onto the desk, kicked off her trainers and headed for her bed. It was then that she saw it. A bright purple envelope, lying on top of her pillow. And scrawled across it were the words:

SUPER SECRET!
FOR ELLY PORTER'S EYES ONLY.

Chapter 2

Elly turned the envelope over. It must be from Aunt Dina: one of her vouchers for 'Aunt-Taught Painting Lessons' or 'Fairy-Cake Baking'. She plopped onto the bed, ripped open the envelope and pulled out a piece of thick handmade paper. No mystery here: her aunt recycled everything—she even made writing paper out of her failed sketches and watercolours, boiling them on the stove until the cottage stank of paper stew.

Elly unfolded the letter and saw that it was a drawing. The paper was carefully torn along

one side. She studied the image, turning it this way and that. She was pretty sure it was supposed to be a map of the island.

It was obviously meant to be a clue in some sort of scavenger hunt. Really, how old did Aunt Dina think she was?

Then Elly noticed the message. Her eyes widened in excitement. *'Meet here tonight at midnight!'* was scrawled in pink glittery ink next to a big red V. Or was it an X with the bottom torn off? And that was all—no signature. A secret midnight meeting. And it definitely wasn't her aunt's handwriting.

So who had left this envelope in her bedroom? The skin on her arms went prickly as she thought about a stranger sneaking up the loft stairs, sliding through the hatch and leaving the mysterious message on her pillow. Elly shivered, then smiled. Grounded or not, she would be at the spot marked on the map at midnight!

The cottage was silent. An hour ago Elly had heard Aunt Dina climbing the stairs to her bedroom. Elly checked her mobile: 11:03. She eased off the bed and crept across the floor, wincing when the floorboards squeaked beneath her feet. She tucked the map in the back pocket of her jeans. Then she climbed onto the desk and struggled with the latch on the casement window. It was stuck, and as she wrenched it free her right foot shot out and kicked the wardrobe. She froze as something clattered to the floor. Sneaking out wasn't as easy as they made it look on TV.

Elly scooted off the desk and crouched beside the hatch, listening. But all was silent below. What had fallen? Using her mobile as a searchlight, she found a small box on the floor. It must have been hidden on top of the wardrobe. It was a jewellery case with initials engraved on the top: SEV. Seraphina Elizabeth Valentine. Her mother!

There was only one thing inside: a silver charm threaded on a chain long enough to wear as a necklace. The charm was about four centimetres long and shaped like a slice of pie with a line down the centre.

Elly held the necklace cupped in her hands, blinking back tears. Her mother had sent her a present from the past. Maybe it was a good omen for tonight's adventure. She fastened the chain around her neck. She needed to hurry now or she'd miss the mysterious rendezvous.

She crawled back on top of the desk

and shoved open the window. A blast of fresh, salt-laden air smacked her in the face. She squeezed backwards through the opening, feet first, until her stomach was propped on the window ledge and her dangling legs brushed the rough stones of the cottage.

Directly below her window was a wooden trellis covered with clematis and honeysuckle. That would be her ladder. She reached out a foot. Not . . . quite. There! As her toes touched something solid, Elly pushed off the window ledge and half slid, half jumped onto the trellis.

One of her feet slipped. She was falling! Hands and feet scrabbled and flailed. Somehow she caught hold and yanked herself to a stop, banging face-first into the leafy green foliage growing up the wall of the cottage. She clung to the trellis, gasping. Then, her arms shaking with the strain, she began the slow, careful climb down. She reached the ground with a sigh of relief.

Elly patted her back pocket to make sure the map was safe, then trotted out of the front gate and away down the lane, dodging between puddles of moonlight and shadow.

Once she was on the lane leading out of the town, she pulled out her mobile and checked the map, using the light from the screen. The cold white glow revealed a path branching off just ahead. It looked as though it climbed up towards the Blake family's mansion.

She tucked the map and her phone back in her pocket. When she reached the fork in the road, she took the winding path up  the hillside. There was just enough moonlight to stop her tripping over boulders sticking out of the peaty soil like half-buried dinosaur bones.

After she had been

walking for about ten minutes, the path narrowed and then disappeared altogether on a granite outcrop. She perched on one of the sloping boulders and fished out her map and mobile. Her phone wouldn't turn on. She must have forgotten to charge it again.

What should she do? Go on and hope for the best, or give up and start back down the hill? The night air was chilly and the sky was beginning to cloud over. She wasn't afraid of the dark, but it was a bit weird being out here on her own. If she had an accident no one would know where she was.

Something rustled in the undergrowth just in front of her. There it was again! There weren't many wild animals on the island. Only hedgehogs and . . . urgh! . . . rats! She leapt to her feet as a dark shape bounded out of the bracken. Something hairy brushed against her leg.

'Aaaah!' Elly screamed.

'Woof!'

In the watery moonlight she saw a small dog standing with its head cocked, watching her. Relief made her grin.

'Hi there!'

The dog gave its tail a single brisk wave, like a windscreen wiper. Then it darted off a metre or so, stopped and looked back. It was obviously waiting for her. Elly hesitated for a second, then tucked away her phone and map and followed. Why not? What did she have to lose? As soon as it saw her coming, the animal darted off down a path she hadn't noticed. A mysterious message, a midnight meeting and now a strange dog, which seemed to be leading her somewhere. *Could this night get any weirder?*

The track sloped downhill. Waist-high bracken rose on either

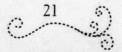

side of her. Elly pushed through it, unpleasantly reminded of her struggle through the sea earlier that afternoon. The path seemed to go on for ever, and she couldn't see the dog any more. *I ought to turn back . . .*

The bracken stopped suddenly and she almost fell out onto an open hillside. *What are those things sticking out of the ground? Th-they look like . . .*

Graves! This had to be a graveyard. Elly threaded her way through the tombstones. Scenes from the zombie movie she had seen last week flicked through her mind. Silly! If there were such things as zombies—and there *weren't*—they wouldn't live . . . uh . . . be undead . . . on boring old Sunday Island.

The dog seemed to have disappeared as mysteriously as it had appeared. She could hear waves crashing onto a beach somewhere ahead. As she turned around to look for a path heading back towards the village, she saw a flash of light coming from the middle of the graveyard.

Elly caught her breath. The light was shining up from the ground . . . from a grave? Was it a ghost? Zombies after all? She ought to get out of here . . . but she had to know.

It was just like all those horror movies where you shout at the stupid idiot alone in the strange house not to go upstairs and investigate the scary noises. Except now she knew why they did it.

Elly crept closer, crouching low between the tombstones. The light flicked out.

'*Help!*'

The cry came from just ahead. 'Could someone help me, please?' A shuffling sound and then another shout. 'Really. A little help here? I'm ruining my manicure.'

That didn't sound like a

zombie. Elly darted forward, tripped over a broken tombstone and did a belly-flop. *'Oof!'* Her hands scrabbled at damp grass. She clawed at the ground and jerked to a stop just as she was about to slide head first into a hole in the ground. A muddy, deep rectangle of a hole. A grave, actually. And, from inside the grave, a face looked up at Elly and screamed.

Chapter 3

Elly lay nose to nose with a girl who looked around her own age. The girl's ear-splitting scream broke off mid-shriek.

'Now that's what I call a dramatic entrance,' she said after a moment, brushing her hair out of her eyes. 'Can you help me out of here?'

'Sure.' Elly wriggled backwards and sat up.

'It's totally gross in this mud! My fave flip-flops are ruined. Is . . .' The girl shuddered. '. . . is this a grave?'

Elly nodded solemnly. 'I think it must be.'

'Urgh!' The girl was chin-deep in the ground. She held out a hand. 'If you pull,

I'll try and climb out.'

'I need to find something to hold on to, or we'll both end up in there.' There was a tombstone just behind her. Elly wrapped one arm around it and held out her other hand. 'Can you reach?'

The girl grabbed her hand and Elly braced herself. It felt as if her arm was being yanked out of its socket as the girl pulled herself out of the grave.

'Oh, look at my flip-flops!' the girl complained. 'Total squelch.' She stamped mud from her feet before turning to Elly. 'But hey, I'm *so* happy to see you! I could have been down there all night!' The girl was tall and slender, with long dark hair. She wore a massive purple handbag slung over a pink denim jacket, jeans and an armful of bangles. And she had a streak of mud right

down the middle of
her face from forehead
to chin, interrupted by
a wide grin.

'Um. You've got mud.'

'So have you.' The girl snorted as she looked
first at Elly then at herself. She rubbed at
her nose, bangles clattering. 'I'm Sierra. I'm
staying with my dad. He lives in a caravan, if
you can believe it. I mean, his whole house
would fit into our lounge at home. And what's
with this island? Half the time I can't even get
a mobile signal.'

'I'm Elly. I'm staying with my aunt.
And—get this—my aunt doesn't believe in
television.'

'Ouch!' Sierra winced in sympathy.

'You haven't seen a dog, have you?' Elly
asked. 'I was following one, but it seems to
have disappeared.'

'You go around at night following dogs?'
Sierra took a careful step backwards.

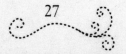

'No.' Elly laughed. 'But even if I did, it's no weirder than hanging out in graveyards at midnight. I got lost up on the hill and this dog showed up and seemed to want me to follow him, so I did. What's your excuse?'

'I found this stupid map someone left in my bedroom as a joke—'

Elly's eyes widened. 'Like this?' She pulled out her own map. 'Have you got a torch?'

Sierra pulled a tiny torch and a folded paper from her jacket pocket.

'Hey! Yours is the other half of mine!' Elly held the bits of paper together. The two maps matched exactly along the torn edge.

'I am getting serious goosebumps.' Sierra's voice was awed.

'It's easy to see where we need to go now.' Elly pointed to the map. 'You coming?'

'I'm sure not staying

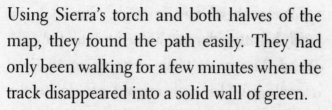

here by myself!' Sierra grinned at Elly and Elly smiled back. Maybe Sunday Island wasn't going to be so bad after all.

Using Sierra's torch and both halves of the map, they found the path easily. They had only been walking for a few minutes when the track disappeared into a solid wall of green.

'It's some sort of hedge. Gosh, it's enormous.' Sierra stared up at the thicket, which towered black against the night sky. 'Why would someone plonk it here?'

'It's not a hedge—it's a maze!' Elly pointed ahead of them, to where an eerie glow rose in the sky. 'And that light seems to be coming from the middle.'

Sierra gasped as she spotted the light. 'Elly, this is getting too weird! I vote we get out of here.'

'But that's "X marks the spot". Aren't you dying to know what this is all about?'

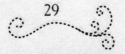

'Ye-es. But I don't like mazes, especially at midnight.'

'We can't turn back now!'

Sierra groaned. 'All right. But if I get killed by one of the island's crazies I'm going to haunt you for all eternity.'

Elly laughed. 'Fair enough.' She took the lead, directing the torch's beam onto the path ahead. The green walls of the maze towered over them. The path curved around to the right and almost immediately another path split off to the left. 'Which way?' Elly asked.

'Left. We should try to keep aiming for the centre.'

They walked deeper into the maze. They tried to head towards the glow of light, but each turn seemed to lead them further away. Elly's heart sank as they stumbled over a stone they had stumbled over at least twice before. 'We're going around in circles.'

Sierra reached out and grabbed Elly's free hand. 'I really don't like this.'

'Don't worry. We're fine.' But she didn't feel fine. The maze was huge. They could be lost in here for hours.

'I've got an idea,' Sierra said and rootled in her handbag. She handed Elly a pot of Purple Passion nail varnish and dug out Glitter Pink for herself. 'Let's paint a few leaves every time we turn so we'll know which paths we've already taken.'

Elly smiled at Sierra. 'Genius!'

They took turns marking each new path. Soon they were in a part of the maze Elly knew they hadn't seen before. This just might work! Ten minutes later they turned a corner and the path widened out into a clearing. It must be the centre of the maze. They had made it!

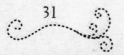

A giant tree stood in the middle of the space. Its thick grey trunk rose out of the mossy ground, looking like stone in the light of the torch. A rope ladder hung down beside the trunk. It was a proper ladder with wooden rungs and it rose five metres into the air to where the first branches sprouted from the trunk. And sitting in the crook of two massive branches was . . .

'Now that,' Sierra said, 'is some tree house!'

It was perfect: large and sturdy and made of wooden boards slatted together. There was a door and a window with light shining through it. Elly turned to Sierra. 'We've got this far. We've gotta go up.'

Sierra steadied the ladder. 'You first.'

Elly was up the ladder in an instant, hauling herself up onto the platform in front of the door. She paused, glanced down at Sierra, then  knocked.

'Woof!'

Footsteps approached and the door was flung open to reveal a girl and the dog from the hill. The girl was wearing combat trousers rolled up to expose sturdy legs and boat shoes. She had an extraordinarily long purple and green scarf looped around and around her neck, an iPod hooked onto her belt, and short, spiky blonde hair. The dog stood at her feet, wagging its tail furiously. The girl grinned at Elly. 'Hi,' she said. 'I'm Tash and this is Mojo. We've been waiting for you.'

Chapter 4

Whoever Tash was, she knew how to make a great hideaway. Cushions to sit on, shelves stuffed with books, iPod speakers, even an old handheld console and some games. The walls were covered with pictures of sailing boats, surfers, dolphins and seals. Elly's mouth watered at the sight of crisp packets, an enormous bar of chocolate and a bag of doughnuts sitting beside a camping lamp on a table.

'I wanted to meet you,' Tash said as she and Elly helped Sierra up the final few rungs on the ladder. 'There's no one else our age who

actually lives here. And I thought a midnight feast would be a great start to our summer on Mystery Island.'

Sierra pointed to a large tear in the knee of her jeans. 'You could have just come to the caravan and said hello.'

Tash laughed. 'What fun would that have been?'

'How did you sneak the invitation into my room?' Elly asked.

Tash arched her eyebrows and smiled wickedly. 'I can't give away all my secrets, now can I? Anyone hungry?' She held out the doughnuts.

Elly fished one out of the bag and took a huge, sugary bite. She was suddenly starving. 'This is great,' she said through her mouthful.

Sierra grabbed a doughnut too. 'Why did you call it Mystery Island?'

'All the islanders call it that,' Tash said. 'We get weird weather. Storms blow up out of nowhere. And we can get some pretty awesome fogs. I have to be careful when I'm out on my boat.' She pointed to a photo of a single-masted dinghy. The name on its prow was 'Mojo'.

'My dad says there's a network of secret tunnels beneath the island, built during World War Two,' Sierra chimed in. 'He's writing a book about it.'

Mojo scampered between the girls, begging for a bite of doughnut. He was a small dog with a rough brown and grey coat and a whiskery face.

'There's supposed to be a sunken pirate ship off Dead Man's Point,' Tash said. 'And the pirates' treasure is meant to be buried somewhere on the island.' She pulled a dog treat out of her pocket and fed it to Mojo.

'This really is a crazy island.' Elly popped

the last of her doughnut into her mouth. 'Like that cemetery on the hill. Sierra fell into an open grave. What is that, tourist control?'

Tash laughed. 'That's Old Man Blake's grave. He put it in his will that he wanted a tombstone erected and a grave dug but never filled. And then he had himself cremated and his ashes sprinkled over the island by helicopter.' Tash lowered her voice. 'Some people say he still haunts the island, looking for someone to take his place in the grave.'

Elly felt the hairs on the back of her neck prickle.

'Well, he may have put it in his will,' said Sierra, 'but that grave is a serious health and safety hazard!'

Elly leant over to grab another doughnut and her mother's pendant slipped from beneath her shirt and plonked into the bag with the doughnuts. As she fished it out, she noticed Sierra staring at her, wide-eyed. 'What's wrong? Have I got jam on my nose?'

'No . . .' Sierra held out her arm. 'But look at this!' She wore a bracelet on her wrist and dangling from it was—

'It's almost the same as mine!' gasped Elly. The charm on Sierra's bracelet had a line down one of the straight edges as well as through the centre, but otherwise it was identical to the one on her mother's necklace. 'Where did you get yours?'

Sierra shrugged. 'I've always had it. My mum got it when she used to stay here years ago. I guess one of the tourist shops sold them.'

Elly nodded, feeling a bit disappointed. 'Makes sense.'

'No,' Tash said, studying the two charms. 'It's a sign.'

'A sign of what?' asked Sierra, rubbing her bracelet nervously up and down her arm.

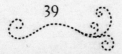

'I don't know,' Tash said and clapped her hands. 'But the island will tell us when it's ready. They don't call this Mystery Island for nothing!'

Elly laughed. Tash was joking, of course. Wasn't she?

They spent the next hour scoffing doughnuts and chocolate, chatting, and listening to a playlist called 'Midnight Music' on Tash's iPod.

Sierra jumped to her feet. 'I love this song,' she said and started to dance.

'You're seriously good!' Tash looked impressed.

'Wow!' Elly liked to dance but Sierra was straight out of a music video.

'I've taken dancing lessons since I was three,' Sierra said. 'I was into ballet when I was little but now I prefer jazz and free style.' She pulled Tash and Elly to their feet.

The girls danced while Mojo scampered around their feet and barked. When the song ended, they fell about laughing. 'I probably need to go home,' Sierra said. 'This has been awesome but Dad'll kill me if he wakes up and I'm missing.'

Elly nodded. 'I'm technically grounded. I'd better go too before my aunt chains me to her cottage like a dog.' She reached down and scratched Mojo behind the ear. 'No offence, Mojo.'

'Let's meet in town after lunch tomorrow,' Tash suggested. 'I know a secret spot where we can go swimming. High Street at one?'

'Sounds great!' Elly and Sierra agreed.

Sierra only screamed twice as Elly and Tash helped her down the rope ladder. Mojo led the way out of the maze before trotting off in the direction of the Blake mansion. Tash

waved goodbye and hurried after him. Elly and Sierra watched them disappear before heading down the hill.

When they reached the outskirts of the town, Sierra gave Elly a quick hug. 'See you tomorrow!' She waved goodbye and Elly saw Sierra's charm bracelet flash in the moonlight.

She watched her new friend stroll off and fingered her pendant. The silver felt cool and mysterious beneath her fingers. Maybe Tash was right. This was a sign. But what did it mean?

Chapter 5

Elly hurried towards town. Clouds scudded across the sky and the moonlight faded in and out. She wished again she had remembered to charge her phone.

She trembled in the chilly wind. It was really late. She'd better be quiet climbing back up to her bedroom. If Aunt Dina caught her, she'd send her straight back to London. A few hours ago, she'd have given anything to go home. But Tash had changed all that with her crazy invitation to a mystery midnight party.

As she approached the cottage, she could

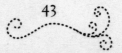

see all the downstairs lights were on. The front door sprang open. She looked up into her aunt's tear-stained face, and felt a sudden rush of guilt.

Her heart thumping, Elly followed Aunt Dina into the cottage.

'What on earth did you think you were doing?' Her aunt plonked a steaming cup of hot chocolate in front of Elly and sat opposite her at the kitchen table, pushing a pile of drawings and paint pots out of the way. 'Drink that up, you must be chilled through.' It was just like Aunt Dina to make her a warm drink even when she was scolding her. It almost made it worse.

'I didn't mean to worry you.' She fished the folded treasure map out of her pocket and handed it to her aunt. 'But it was the most amazing

thing ever. I found out
there are two other girls
living on the island. Tash
sent me this, and I met Sierra
in the graveyard up the hill. We had to find
our way through a maze, then we found Tash
in her tree house and had a midnight feast.
I'm sorry. I should have asked permission,
but . . . I was scared you'd say no, or want to
come along to make sure it was safe and that
would have ruined it.' How could she make
her aunt understand how important this was
to her? 'I had such a great time tonight, Auntie
Dee.' Desperation made her blurt: 'I bet you
would have done the same thing if you were
my age.'

Her aunt's frown didn't budge, not one
millimetre.

Just when she'd made some friends and had
started to think her summer wouldn't be so
horrible. 'Please. Don't send me home.'

Her aunt had spread the map out on the

table. Now she looked up and shook her head. Her face was solemn. 'Your friend Tash needs drawing lessons. Perhaps you'd like to invite her and Sierra around some afternoon when I'm not too busy and I'll give all of you an art lesson.'

'I can stay?' Elly shrieked and jumped to her feet, making the cup of hot chocolate wobble dangerously, and gave Aunt Dina a power-hug.

Her aunt hugged her back. She reached up and smoothed the hair away from Elly's eyes. 'I'm happy you've made some friends. I know you've been bored here with just me. But . . .' Her face grew stern again. '. . . you pull one more stunt like this and I'll sprout wings like a jumbo jet and fly you home myself! And that is a promise.'

The next morning Aunt Dina and Elly picnicked in

the tiny back garden, carrying muffins, orange juice and an enormous pot of tea out to the tiled table Aunt Dina had made a few years ago when mosaic was in fashion. The garden was full of sunshine and the scent of lavender, thyme and rosemary, mixed with the smell of the sea.

Aunt Dina took a huge bite of one of her homemade muffins. 'These are excellent, if I do say so myself. I thought peach and cinnamon would work. Yum!' Her voice took on a sad note. 'Your mum was mad keen on peaches.'

'Peach cobbler,' Elly remembered aloud. She touched the pendant around her neck. She had slept in it.

'Elly, what's that?' Her aunt's voice was suddenly sharp.

'I found it in my bedroom.' Slowly, Elly unfastened the pendant, hoping she wasn't

in trouble again already. 'It was on top of the wardrobe in a jewellery case with my mother's initials on it.'

Aunt Dina took the necklace with gentle hands and sat looking at it for several moments. 'I haven't seen this for years,' she said at last, and handed the necklace back to Elly. 'Phee wore it all the time when she was your age.' A wobbly chime rang out. 'Is that the doorbell?'

Her aunt plonked her teacup down and disappeared through the kitchen door. She returned a few moments later with a visitor.

'Hi, there!' Sierra waved a bangled arm. 'Hope it's OK to pop by.'

'It's great. Aunt Dina already knows about our midnight meeting.' Elly pointed to the shrinking pile of muffins. 'Grab one quick, Sierra, before I eat them all.'

'Yes, join us.' Aunt Dina

pulled out another chair.

'Thanks.' Sierra perched.

She bit into a muffin. 'They're scrummy! I'm starving, as usual. Dad calls me his bottomless pit. I mean, how flattering is that, being compared to a big hole in the ground?' She made a comical face and turned to Aunt Dina. Elly could tell her aunt had taken a liking to her friend.

'That's how we met,' Sierra continued. 'Did Elly tell you? I was in a deep dark muddy hole and she pulled me out. Too late for my fave flip-flops, though. They are so ruined. Good thing I always travel with another pair—a dozen actually.' She shook her head and stuck out a long, elegant foot. Her toenails were painted silver and she wore flimsy, jewelled flip-flops.

Aunt Dina choked on a bite of muffin and took a quick sip of tea. 'Well, I certainly would avoid muddy holes in those.'

'Oh, I will.' Sierra nodded her head solemnly. 'I'm meeting up with Tash and going for a swim. Can Elly come with me, please?' She patted her handbag. 'I've packed extra sun block.'

'After last night Elly should be doubly grounded,' said Aunt Dina.

'It was all my fault!' Sierra said quickly. 'I mean, once we were at the tree house, we were all having such a good time. Elly said she ought to get back so you wouldn't worry, but I begged her to stay longer. I'm really sorry.'

'She shouldn't have gone out in the first place without telling me.'

'Oh, I know!' Sierra nodded, the picture of total sincerity. 'But we got these crazy letters about treasure and . . . well, can you really blame us?' Sierra smiled at Aunt Dina, turning the wattage on full, and Elly saw her aunt begin to melt.

'You said you wanted me to make friends,' Elly added.

'Oh, very well.' Aunt Dina shook her head. 'The two of you are too much for me. But you make sure you are back here by six o'clock prompt, young lady, or in the name of chocolate, crochet and my great-aunt Lulu's pet crocodile, you'll have used up your last chance!'

The high street was a jumble of tourists in bright shirts and shorts, with sunglasses and loud, holiday voices. Elly and Sierra weaved their way through the crowd, looking for Tash.

'There she is.' Sierra stuck both arms in the air and whooped. Tash ran across the road to meet them, her spiky blonde head dodging through the crowd.

'Superb. You guys made it! Now we just

have to find Mojo and we can abandon town. The grockle invasion force is too strong,' Tash said, with a glance at the groups of tourists crowded around the shop windows. She led them to the town square, with its central fountain and flower beds, old stone shops and houses. Visitors occupied clusters of umbrellaed tables, sipping coffee and eating pastries.

'Odds on he'll be in here,' Tash said, heading for the ice-cream parlour.

'Clever dog!' said Sierra, as she and Elly pushed through the shop door to find Mojo licking the last of something that looked suspiciously like raspberry ripple out of a bowl on the floor. 'Make mine pistachio.'

The lady shopkeeper laughed. 'Is that a plain cone or chocolate?'

Sierra chose a plain cone for her two scoops

of pistachio, Tash had double chocolate chip in a chocolate cone and Elly, after a long struggle, decided on a chocolate cone with one scoop of raspberry ripple and another of sticky toffee pudding. They strolled towards the harbour, concentrating on eating the ice cream before the sun could melt it. Mojo followed close behind. Soon they passed the sailing club. Rows of dinghies and small yachts sat on trailers, the breeze setting their rigging jingling in a constant clatter even louder than Sierra's bangles.

'That's my dinghy there,' Tash said, pointing to a sturdy blue sailing boat. I'll take you out in it soon. We could explore some of the uninhabited islands.'

'Excellent!' Elly admired the little boat. 'I've always wanted to learn to sail!'

'Hmm.' Sierra frowned. 'It looks awfully small to take out on that big ol' sea!'

'Don't worry!' Tash laughed. 'I've been sailing since I was eight. I know the coastline around here better than most of the fishermen. The only thing you'll have to do is remember to duck when I jibe or the boom will crack you on the head.'

'Boom? Jibe? Is that a new dance?' Sierra boogied up the path ahead of them, all long legs and smooth moves.

Tash led them uphill at a killer pace. Soon all three girls were too out of breath to talk, let alone dance. They climbed above the bracken onto an open hillside. The heather was blooming. Bees tumbled in the purple and orange blossom, tossed by the wind, which was stronger up here. It whipped the girls' hair away from their faces. A seagull swirled high overhead, riding the thermals. The warmth of the sun and the smell of the sea and heather flooded over Elly. It was the first time since her mother's death that she had felt like this: at peace and just . . . happy.

Chapter 6

The girls climbed to a plateau on the hillside. The coast of the mainland stretched in front of them, headlands grey with granite between curves of sandy beaches. The sea was turquoise near land, cobalt further out.

Tash turned to Elly and Sierra, her eyes shining. 'I never get tired of it.' She shrugged. 'Except all winter when it never stops raining!'

Now the girls headed down the other side of the hill. Two-thirds of the way down, the path entered the dappled shade of a beech wood. Almost at once, Mojo darted off, barking and growling, into the wood. 'Mojo! Here, boy!'

With a grunt of annoyance, Tash ran after him. Elly and Sierra followed, stumbling through the undergrowth.

'Wait!' Sierra cried. 'My flip-flops keep coming off.'

'Don't you have any trainers?' Elly slid to a stop and turned to see Sierra hopping on one foot, collecting the offending footwear.

'Trainers? *Quelle horreur!*' Sierra slid the flip-flop back on and smiled. 'Come on, bet I can run faster than you, even in these.'

They raced, sliding over the slippery ground, and soon caught up with Tash. She had taken off the red scarf she was wearing for a belt, tied it to Mojo's collar and was tugging the dog away from a clearing. 'We should get out of here,' she said, pointing over her shoulder to a ramshackle shack in the middle of the clearing.

'What is this place?'
Elly stared at the
shack. Sunlight washed
into the clearing, showing
a pile of neatly stacked firewood
and a small vegetable garden, the dark peaty
soil hoed in rows. Hanging from the roof of
the half-rotten porch were bunches of herbs
and onions, drying.

'A hermit lives here. He's been here for
years, but no one sees him much any more.
I don't specially want to meet him—they say
he's bonkers.'

Tash had to drag a whining Mojo, but once
back on the path, he seemed to forget what
had so interested him in the old shack and
trotted happily after them.

The beech trees gave way to a row of
windblown pines and the edge of a cliff. It
dropped twenty metres to a foreshore tumbled
with boulders and rock pools. Beyond that
lay a perfect crescent of silvery sand, glinting

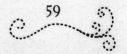

in the hot sunshine. A rocky headland curved gently around the small bay, offering protection from the open sea.

'Mirror Cove,' Tash said. 'The best swimming spot on the island. It's so far from town most of the tourists never get up here. Most of the locals can't be bothered either — you have to climb down the cliff.'

'What?' yelped Sierra. She looked longingly down at the warm sand and gently lapping waves. Then she looked at the rocks and shuddered. 'I hate heights.'

'Don't look down,' suggested Elly. 'You can go on your bum!'

'And ruin a perfectly good pair of shorts? No way.' Sierra kicked off her flip-flops and stuffed them in her handbag. 'Although this won't do my pedicure any favours!'

'Pedicure?' Tash had untied

her scarf from Mojo's collar.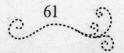

'She means her silver toenail varnish.'

'Pedicure!' Sierra corrected. '"Toenail" is *so* unattractive.'

Tash knotted her scarf into a belt and swung herself over the edge of the cliff. She half slid, half jumped down the steep granite slope. Mojo followed, tail in full windscreen wiper mode. Looking slightly grim, Sierra lowered herself down the track worn through the boulders, clinging with hands and bare feet. Elly followed.

'Hey, give us a hand here,' Sierra called. She had reached the top of a two-metre drop of smooth rock. Tash had carried Mojo past this part. Elly knelt, bracing herself, and gripped Sierra's hand. Her friend took a deep breath and lowered herself down the wall, letting go of Elly's hand when she reached solid ground. 'Thanks!' she said, shooting a wan smile at Elly. 'That wasn't so bad.'

They were past the steepest part now and the rest was easy. Elly followed the others down, pausing at the rock pools while Tash showed them sea anemones, limpets and crabs. They took their shoes off and padded over warm sand to the water's edge. Mirror Cove rang with excited barking when Mojo spotted the dark head of a seal bobbing in the water. After listening to the row for a few minutes, the seal ducked under water and disappeared.

'That's what I want to do,' Tash said. 'Swim!'

'You bet.' Elly peeled off her shorts and T-shirt. She'd worn her two-piece underneath: a compromise between the bikini she'd asked for and the one-piece Aunt Dina had nearly insisted upon. Tash was wearing a sporty two-piece but Sierra, whom she'd expected to see in something tiny, trendy and totally impractical, was wearing a sleek red Speedo suit. 'Whoa, Sierra!'

Sierra patted the swimsuit fondly. 'I swim for my school. Fashion is fun, but hey, swimming is for real.' She pulled off her bangles and dangling earrings and piled them on top of her clothes. 'Treasure, Mojo,' she said to the dog. 'Guard it with your life!'

Mojo gave her a doggy grin and immediately ran off to investigate the base of the cliff.

'Deserter!' Sierra called after him.

Giggling, the girls waded out into the chilly water. The waves lapping around Elly's legs seemed so different from the ones that had nearly drowned her on the causeway. She pushed away the memory, took a deep breath and dived right under. She kicked into a steady crawl and was soon warm enough to enjoy the feel of her arms and legs pushing her through the water. When she reached the

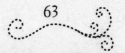

middle of Mirror Cove, Elly looked around for the others.

'Hi there!' Tash surfaced next to her, looking for a moment just like Mojo as she shook the water from her hair. 'Look at Sierra go!' She pointed seawards and Elly bobbed round in the water in time to see a streak of red power through the gentle waves, do a dolphin-like turn and start back towards them. 'Wow,' Tash sounded wistful. 'And I thought *I* was a good swimmer!'

The sound of Mojo, barking frantically, floated out to them.

'What's he up to now?' Tash peered towards the shore. 'I'd best check.' She struck out towards the beach. Elly caught Sierra's eye and they dived into the water at the same moment. Sierra reached the beach first, followed closely by a worried

Tash. Elly's feet hit
sand and she staggered
ashore after her friends.
Mojo's barks had become hysterical.

Elly spotted the dog just in time to see him wriggle into a small hole and disappear.

'Mojo!' screamed Tash. 'No! Come back!'

Chapter 7

When Elly reached them, Tash and Sierra were kneeling at the spot where Mojo had vanished. The cliff face seemed as full of holes as Dad's favourite Emmental cheese.

'I can hear him barking!' Tash's voice was tense. 'Here, Mojo! Come here, boy!' But the dog's barking only got more frantic.

'Maybe he's stuck,' Sierra said.

'Probably just stubborn.' Tash groaned. 'The whole island sits on a honeycomb of caves. If he wanders off down a tunnel he could end up lost for ever.' She picked up a pointed rock and began to chip away

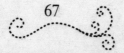

at the hole. Elly found another rock and helped. Sierra ran off and came back a few moments later with a flat piece of driftwood. She used it to scrape away the debris, keeping the entrance clear and not mentioning her manicure once. The girls worked steadily, Tash calling constantly to Mojo, who barked and whined in reply.

'I can feel a breeze inside here!' Tash cried. 'It must be the entrance to a cave.'

They hammered and dug with new determination. Suddenly the hole collapsed in a shower of mud and shingle.

'Oh no!' Tash looked ready to cry.

'It'll be OK,' Elly soothed. They began to clear the rubble. As they were pushing the last of it away, a whiskery face poked out of the hole. 'Woof!' Mojo jumped out, barking in delight. His short wiry coat was

covered with dirt and
small pebbles but Tash
didn't seem to mind. She
scooped up the small dog
and hugged him as he licked her face.

'You stupid dog!' Tash's voice sounded
wobbly. 'Don't ever do that again! You could
have been killed.'

Mojo ducked his furry head and gave Tash
a woeful look.

'Oh, look at him, making up to you!'
Sierra cried, standing up and dusting off her
swimsuit. 'He'll be batting his eyelashes next!'

'Border terriers are too clever by half
sometimes,' Tash said with a sigh. 'He always
has to stick his nose into everything. Oh well,
anyone for another swim?'

'Sure!' Elly glanced at the sky. Her watch
was with her clothes, but judging by the sun
it was still early afternoon. 'Just don't let me
forget—I have to be back by six.'

They splashed in the cove for what felt like

69

an hour. When her legs and arms began to feel heavy, Elly returned to the beach. She lay face up on the sand with her eyes closed, the bright sunshine turning the insides of her eyelids white, and listened to Tash and Sierra splashing and shrieking. Soon they joined her and all three girls lay drowsing in the sunshine, Mojo a snoring heap beside them.

'*What are you doing on my beach?*'

The voice jerked Elly awake. She sat up, trying to see where it had come from. Sierra was already kneeling in the sand. Tash had jumped to her feet and was struggling to keep hold of a frantic Mojo.

'There!' Elly pointed. 'On top of the cliff, just by the path!'

A scruffy old man with long white hair and an even longer beard stood on the edge of the cliff. One arm was raised and he was actually shaking his fist at them.

'Get off my beach!'
shouted the old man.
'You have no right!
Always three girls! Why
do you keep coming back?
Always three girls!' He was waving both fists
in the air now.

Elly's heart was thudding so fast she felt
sick. 'Who is that guy?'

'I think it's the hermit,' Tash said. She knelt
down and grabbed Mojo by the collar. The
dog's barks rang through the air, shrill and
frantic above the old man's voice. 'And this
isn't his beach. He can't frighten us off like
this and I'm going to tell him so!'

'Wait,' Sierra grabbed Tash's arm. 'He could
be dangerous. Let's just ignore him.'

'No way!' Tash glared up at the old man,
now nearly dancing in fury on top of the cliff.
'I'm not scared of—'

'Tash? Um, Tash?' Sierra interrupted. She
was pointing out to sea.

Elly slowly got to her feet, shivering. 'I've never seen anything . . .' Her voice faded as she stared at a giant grey wall of fog rolling swiftly towards them.

Before she could draw another breath, the fog was all around her, cold and clammy. She could only see a few centimetres in front of her nose. Elly felt a wave of claustrophobia sweep over her. She heard Sierra give a tiny scream. Mojo began whimpering and she could hear Tash making soothing noises somewhere to her right. Only the hermit continued to shout as if nothing had happened.

'*Leave my beach alone!*' The old man's voice sounded even weirder in the fog. Muffled and far away. '*Leave this place . . .*' the voice faded away.

Cold fingers crept up Elly's back. 'Tash? Sierra? Are you there?' 'Over here!' Sierra's voice sounded miles away.

'Where?' Elly groped, hands out, stumbling over the sand. Sierra had been right beside her. But now she was gone. Elly's heart was going at a hundred miles an hour. She was scared and she didn't mind who knew it. 'I can't find you!'

'Hold on!' The sound of Tash's voice, calm and totally normal, made Elly feel loads better. 'These fogs happen all the time. Don't let it freak you out. They usually go as quickly as they come. Just wait it out.'

'Can we get together, please?' Sierra's voice sounded small and nervous.

'Not a good idea,' said Tash. 'The fog distorts sound so it's best to stay put. We're perfectly safe here. Let's sit down and talk until the fog leaves.'

'If it ever does . . .' Sierra muttered. But Elly heard the sound of the others settling into the sand, and she sat down too. The fog was cold and damp but at least the sand was

73

still warm from the sun.

'Do you know that old guy, Tash?' Sierra asked.

'No.'

'But he kept on about three girls,' Elly said.

'I don't understand.' Tash sounded puzzled. 'I used to come here sometimes by myself, when I was younger. But since I've been sailing I mostly go to a beach on one of the smaller islands if I want to swim. In the summer I like to take the boat out every day if I can. It must be three other girls . . .' Tash's voice faded doubtfully. They all knew there were no other girls on the island except tourists. 'Well,' she continued, 'I think it's a sign. Has to be. I mean, that old nutter shouting about three girls and now the fog.'

'A sign of what?' Elly asked. No one answered, except Mojo, who barked.

Elly didn't know how long it took before the fog began to clear, but it seemed for ever. She kept waiting for the hermit's voice to blare out at them. Instead, the grey mist slowly faded, leaving pale wisps drifting above the beach like ghosts. Elly found herself sitting facing the sea. Somehow she had turned herself completely around.

'It's like some weird dream,' said Sierra. 'Time warp and everything. It feels late.'

'Oh no!' Elly raced to where she had dumped her clothes and tugged her watch out of her shorts pocket. She gasped when she saw the time. 5.31. 'I'm doomed! I've got to be home in thirty minutes and there's no way I can make it. If I mess up again my aunt will send me back to London.' It felt as if someone had kicked her in the stomach.

'Come on!' Tash jumped to her feet. 'I think I know a way.'

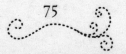

They scrambled into their clothes, gathered the rest of their stuff and ran for the cliff. Mojo and Tash seemed to fly up it. Elly leapt from rock to rock. She reached the vertical wall and pulled herself up using finger and toe holds in the rock. Then it grew a bit easier. She was puffing by the time she reached the top of the cliff. Just as she was about to pull herself over the edge, she heard Sierra scream.

Elly twisted round to see her friend dangling by her hands at the top of the vertical drop. 'Hold on!' Elly shouted. She slid free-form downhill. She could hear Tash following.

'I can't!' Sierra cried. Elly saw one of her hands begin to slip, and then grab hold again. Elly's heart was pounding in her head. *Don't let her fall!* she prayed. But she had prayed for her mother too. She leapt to the next boulder, slithered down the last few metres.

Elly lowered herself onto her stomach, grabbed one of Sierra's hands and began to pull.

'I can't find a foothold!' Sierra cried. Elly could hear her feet scrabbling against the rock.

'Relax. Feel for it!'

Tash thudded down beside Elly and grabbed Sierra's other hand with both of hers. 'We'll pull you up,' she called.

It wasn't easy. Sierra was slender, but she was solid muscle and taller than either of them. They struggled but finally pulled Sierra to safety. She collapsed in a heap beside them.

'It's OK.' Sierra's voice was quivering, but she sat up and stuck out her feet, pointing her toes ballet-style. 'I didn't lose the flip-flops!'

Chapter 8

By the time they were back on the cliff top, happy and sad were all mixed up in Elly's head. Sierra was safe but it was now only fifteen minutes till Aunt Dina's curfew. Even if she ran the whole way, she couldn't make it back in time.

Tash turned to her. 'I can get you back super fast, but it could be dangerous.'

'Anything!'

Did Tash have a quad bike stashed somewhere?

'You mean, more dangerous than falling off a cliff?' Sierra frowned at Tash. 'It would be

good to keep the girl in one piece, boss.'

'Come on. Tell me!' Elly couldn't bear the thought of being stuck in the flat all summer, knowing that her new friends were having fun without her.

'Follow me!' Tash led them inland at breakneck speed. In a few minutes they reached what locals called the River. For most of its course it was a shallow stream tumbling over rocks. Here it deepened and began to rush down the hillside. Elly skidded to a stop on the river bank.

'So, is she gonna turn into a fish and swim downstream or what?' Sierra asked.

'Almost!' Tash jogged over to a pile of bracken beneath one of the willows. 'Give me a hand!'

They scooped up armfuls of dead and dying bracken and tugged them to one side,

reveiling something
that looked like a
homemade sledge without
runners. Tash lifted one end. 'Help me pull it
to the riverbank.'

Elly and Sierra grabbed the other end. It
only took a moment to carry it over to the
water. Sierra stepped back and frowned. 'I
hope that's not what I think it is,' she said.

'A raft.' Tash gazed at it with pride. 'This bit
of the river is like a water slide. You could ride
down, see? I made the raft a few weeks ago,
but I haven't used it yet.'

'Wonder why?' Sierra's voice was sarky.

'Where does the river come out?' Elly was
surprised she sounded so calm. Her stomach
was twisting itself into a pretzel and her
mouth had gone dry and cottony.

'Near the caravan site where the river runs
into the lake.' Tash reached down to stroke
Mojo, who was sniffing the raft. 'But maybe
Sierra's right. I bottled it the other day—

didn't have the nerve. Forget it, Elly. We'll go and talk to your aunt. I'll explain—'

'Sierra and I only just managed to get her to let me come out today. If I mess up again that will be it.' Elly took a deep breath. 'I'm gonna do it.'

Sierra caught her arm. 'That thing could break apart. Or you could fall off and crack your head open on a rock!'

Elly gave her friends a shaky smile. 'I'm going.' She climbed onto the raft, lying face down and grabbing the rope hand-holds.

'Hold on tight!' Tash's voice sounded excited. Elly turned to look at Sierra. Her face was white but when she caught Elly's eye she nodded and knelt to help push the raft. It scraped over the ground, lurching and pausing. Then it seemed to get stuck.

'Muscle it!' shouted Sierra,

sounding strangely fierce.

There were groans and squeals from both her friends and then Elly found herself sliding over the edge of the riverbank and into the river with a huge, drenching splash.

The raft shuddered, tried to spin and hurtled into the riverbank. It scraped and bumped, then gathered speed until it began to race downstream, going faster with every second.

It was like riding a bouncing, bucking bed—but without a mattress. Elly held on as the raft did its best to shake her off. She was flopping up and down on her belly like a landed fish. Water sheered over the front of the raft into her face.

She rushed down the steep hill on the back of the river. And then she was slowing, the raft no longer shaking like a crazed animal but bobbing gently. Elly blinked water out of her

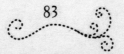

eyes and caught a glimpse of the caravan site. She had made it!

The river widened out into a lake. The raft was circling now, swirling gently round and round. Elly slid into the water and swam for the muddy lake edge, trembling with adrenaline and cold. She scrambled ashore. Her trainers splattered water with every step as she sprinted towards town. She had no idea how long the wild ride down the river had taken. Was it too late already? She looked at her watch. It had stopped. The river ride had claimed a casualty.

It was about a five-minute run into town. Elly reached the cottage gasping and clutching a stitch in her side. She kicked off her trainers in the hall, eased open the sitting room door and checked the clock on the mantelpiece. 5:57! She had made it home

with three minutes to
spare. Now she had
to get out of these wet
clothes before Aunt Dina
saw them.

Cooking noises clattered from the kitchen.

'Hi! I'm back!' Elly called. 'Just gonna have
a shower.' She shut the door and raced for the
stairs. She had reached the first floor when
Aunt Dina's voice followed her.

'Elly? Did you have a good time? Hurry
with that shower and come down. Supper's
nearly ready.'

'Mmm.' Elly scooped another ginormous
spoonful of lasagne onto her plate. She took
a huge mouthful and shut her eyes as she
chewed. Rich, cheesy, tomatoey heaven.
Lasagne and salad were beginning to fill up
the hollow space that seemed to reach from
her toes to her chin.

'Steady-on, El!' Aunt Dina shook her head

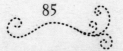

in mock horror. 'You must have swum the channel to raise that sort of appetite. Good thing I made banoffee pie for desert.'

'Have a good day in the studio then?'

'How did you guess?' Aunt Dina grinned back at her. 'That red painting is finally starting to work. I was just about ready to boil it up for scrap. *And* I got a call from the gallery. They sold two watercolours and one acrylic today. Halle-flippin-luja, the season has officially started!'

'Hey, we're rich!'

'We are indeed. Bless our dear tourists. I'd take you shopping on the mainland this week but the gallery wants more blue paintings. It seems blue is in this year.'

'So much for your red painting then.' Elly waved a lasagne-laden fork dismissively. 'That was a waste of paint!'

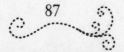

'You want that pie or not? I'm quite happy to eat the whole—' Her aunt broke off at the sound of a dog barking at the front door.

'Mojo!' Elly sprang up from her chair. Why hadn't Tash rung the bell? She dashed to the door and pulled it open. No Tash. Only Mojo, set square on four sturdy legs, his tail a blur.

'Who is it, Elly?' Aunt Dina had followed her. 'I know that dog! I see him everywhere.'

'It's Tash's dog. And look! He's got something tied to his collar.' Elly knelt and Mojo leapt up and began licking her face. 'Urgh. Stop it, Mojo. I love you too, but I need to see what this is. Sit! Good dog. Sit!'

'I don't think this one's been to obedience school.' Her aunt's voice was dry. She knelt beside Elly and took hold of Mojo's collar. Mojo stopped bouncing and looked up at Aunt Dina with his head cocked sideways. 'Stop acting the fool, young man. I've got the measure of you!' And it seemed she had, for Mojo sat statue-still as Elly unfastened the small pouch attached to his collar with a Velcro strap.

'It's a letter from Tash!' Elly had unfolded a square of shiny turquoise paper. Written on it were the words:

Super Secret Meeting!!!
Sunday House
Tomorrow morning at 10:30 am
rsvp via Mojo

'Sunday House? That's the Blake mansion, isn't it? You didn't tell me your friend Tash was Old Man Blake's granddaughter.' Aunt Dina kept a firm hold of Mojo's collar, as the dog seemed to want to scamper away now he had made his delivery.

'She never told us her last name.'

'I suppose you want to go to this super-secret meeting, do you?'

'Course I do. Tash will have invited Sierra too. Please, can I go, Aunt Dina?'

'Find a bit of paper to write a note. Quick now, before this gorgeous little devil of a dog tricks me into letting go of his collar. He'll be off, RSVP or no RSVP!'

Once Elly's note had been carried off into the summer evening by the impatient Mojo, Elly and her aunt took their banoffee pie and sat in the sitting room, listening to Aunt Dina's favourite mix of jazz, blues and nineties pop songs.

'Who was Old Man Blake?' Elly was trying to adjust her idea of sunny, down-to-earth Tash to include rich parents, scary old mansions and empty graves.

'He was your friend's grandfather. He was some sort of inventor and had a reputation for being eccentric. By all accounts he never got over his wife's death. When she died he sent his young daughter away to boarding school and shut himself up in that big old house. He lived there all alone for years.

'Sunday House is supposed to be stuffed full of his inventions. It was left standing empty for years before his daughter and her husband John Reynolds moved back in. The place got a reputation for being haunted.' Aunt Dina shot a worried look at Elly. A rich, crazy old inventor and a haunted mansion! Elly felt a delicious shiver run down her back.

The sun was setting as Elly climbed the loft ladder to her bedroom. The swimming, the hermit and mysterious fog, the ride down the river on Tash's homemade raft — they were all jumbled together in her head and

she wondered if she
would be able to
sleep. The last rays of
sunlight stretched across
the floor.

Sunsets on the island were beautiful but
brief. Once the sun went below the rim of
the sea, darkness fell with a suddenness that
was almost spooky. Elly stood at the window
watching the indigo sky vibrate behind stripes
of gold, purple and red. The sun was a mere
sliver of orange now, dropping rapidly into the
sea. One last fiery flash and it disappeared.
Elly's bedroom grew dark. She yawned. It
would be weird tomorrow, seeing Tash and
knowing all that stuff about her grandad.

Without intending to, Elly found herself
looking through the other window, up the
big hill, towards the spot where the Blake
mansion must be. From this distance, the
mansion was just visible. Most of the house
lay in darkness. But right at the top a faint

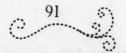

yellowish glow flickered from window to window. Someone—or something—was moving slowly and steadily around and around the attics of Sunday House.

Chapter 9

After breakfast, Elly decided to pick up Sierra before heading to Sunday House.

As she approached Sierra's caravan, she heard the sound of raised voices. Sierra and her dad were rowing. Elly froze, unsure whether to knock on the door or not.

'Why do I have to think of everything? I mean, who's the parent here? Seriously!'

'Look, I'm sorry, Sierra. For god's sake, stop shouting at me. So I forgot to get food in. *¿Cuál es el problema?* Be a sweetie and go fetch some doughnuts and coffee. We can—'

'I'm going out with my friends. If you're

hungry get your own food!'

'*Princesa*, please. I've got a book to write.'

'You care more about your stupid book than you do about me!'

'That's not—'

'What about dinner last night at the Anchor? I waited for ages.'

'*Lo siento!*'

'You *always* forget! Well, now I'm going to forget you for a while.'

The caravan door crashed open and Sierra spilled out, all flying dark hair and clattering bangles. She slammed the door shut with a thud that echoed over the lake. Then she sprinted down the caravan steps onto the path. When she saw Elly she slid to a stop and her angry frown dissolved into embarrassment.

Elly ran forward and gave her friend a big hug. Sierra squeezed back, then pulled away, sniffing.

94

'Thanks. But I'm fine. Really.' She grabbed Elly's hand. 'Let's get out of here.'

They circled the lake, marching along the peaty path. Sierra couldn't seem to get away fast enough. 'Sorry about that,' she said, after a while.

'It's OK.'

'No. It's not. My dad is driving me crazy. He's writing this stupid book on island history. And he doesn't remember to do any normal things. This was supposed to be our special summer together.'

'You live with your mother, don't you?'

'During term time. I'm supposed to stay with Dad in the holidays, but last year he couldn't be bothered. *That* was a different book. This summer was supposed to make up for it, but as far as I can see I'm only here to do his cooking and cleaning. He wants a housekeeper, not a daughter. Well, I'm fed

up with it. With both of them. They're SO childish!'

'What d'you mean?'

'My parents. Mum's OK most of the time. I mean, she lives for shopping but, hey, nothing wrong with that.' Sierra gave her a weak smile and Elly tried to grin back. She still felt a scary sort of emptiness and jealousy whenever anyone talked about their mum. She ignored the feeling and gave Sierra's hand a squeeze.

'They can't even talk to each other on the phone.' Sierra shook her head in disgust. 'I mean, they were childhood sweethearts and now they can't even speak except through me. Unbelievable! If I ever get that dumb just hit me on the head, get a taxidermist to stuff me, and put me in a museum next to the dodo, OK?'

Despite the sad feeling, Elly had to laugh. 'You're totally crazy!'

'All the best people are.' This time, Sierra smiled as if she meant it.

'Oh, I almost forgot,' Sierra said, rummaging in her massive purple handbag. 'A little gift for you!' She handed Elly a pair of electric green flip-flops with thick, grippy soles. 'Free your toes!'

'How did you know I love green?' Elly kicked off her trainers, which had never really recovered from the river ride, and slipped on the flip-flops. Rainbow-coloured straps criss-crossed her foot. 'These are amazing!' Elly said, dancing on the shoes' spongy soles.

'We'll talk pedicure later. I've got the equipment here.' Sierra patted her handbag. 'I can carry your trainers. Masses of room.'

'You can carry a whole shoe shop in there.' Elly watched in awe as the bag swallowed her trainers with ease.

'That's the idea.' Sierra grinned. 'Wait till you see what I've got for Tash.'

The front door of Sunday House swung open the moment the doorbell stopped ringing. Tash stood there, looking normal and Tash-like even though now Elly knew she was actually a Blake heiress.

'Thanks for having us over!' Elly said as Tash showed them into a massive hall. It was like one of Mum's film sets: dark and gloomy, with a high ceiling where the plastering was done in patterns. The walls were covered with faded wallpaper straight out of a BBC costume drama, and there were speckled mirrors and dark oily looking paintings everywhere.

'I got you a prezzie!' Sierra pulled a pair of sparkling purple jelly flip-flops from her handbag.

'Wow,' Tash said. 'Those are amazing.' She slipped them on her bare feet.

'Never underestimate the power of stellar footwear!'

Sierra beamed. 'I was thinking pedicure. I've got loads of nail varnish with me—'

'Maybe later,' Tash interrupted. 'I've got something to show you.' She held up her fist and then slowly opened her fingers—Elly saw a glint of silver.

'Hey!' Sierra held up her left wrist, where the charm bracelet was half-hidden beneath an armful of bangles.

'But that's . . .' Elly couldn't believe it: Tash was holding a badge made from a silver charm, and it was the reverse image of Sierra's.

'I found this last night.' Tash's eyes glowed with excitement. She waved her badge at them. 'Take yours off. I've got an idea.'

'Uh oh.' Sierra shook her head in mock horror. 'Another sign?' But she unfastened her charm bracelet and held it out. Elly slipped the pendant from around her neck.

She felt strangely reluctant to let go of it, but when Tash held out her hand, Elly dropped the necklace into her palm.

Tash strode to a table standing opposite the door and laid out the charms. On its dark, polished surface they shone like triplet moons. Elly watched, feeling a fluttering grow in her stomach as Tash's sturdy fingers slid the silver shapes together, apart, switched them around. And then, with a slight clicking noise, the three pieces slotted together.

'Yes!' Tash punched the air. She stepped away so they could look.

'A peace symbol?' Sierra's voice was incredulous as she leant over the table.

Elly reached out a finger and touched the silver circle divided by an upside down Y.

Her mother's pendant had disappeared—fitting into the other two charms

like a puzzle piece. It gave her an odd feeling
in her chest.

'But how come we all . . .' Sierra trailed off
and straightened up. She gazed from Elly to
Tash and her eyes grew large with excitement.

'A mystery! This is getting seriously fun. What do you know, Tash?'

'When you guys showed me your charms I knew I'd seen something like them before. But I couldn't remember where until last night. The attic. There's no light up there and I had to use a torch. It took me hours to find it.'

Elly smiled to herself. So *that* explained the ghostly lights she had seen last night!

'But it's so strange,' Sierra blurted. 'Why do we each have one?'

'What do you know about yours, Sierra?' Tash asked.

Sierra shrugged. 'It used to belong to my mum, but she never said much about it, except she got it on the island. After I saw Elly's I asked my dad about it. He said he remembered Mum wearing it when he met her. That was ages ago—they were like fifteen. What about you, Elly?'

Elly's throat went tight, the way it always did when someone asked about her mum. She shrugged and managed, 'Sort of the same.'

'I think I can solve The Mystery of the Silver Charms,' Tash announced in a spooky voice and paused.

'Tell us!' Sierra cried.

'It's more fun to show you. Follow me.'

Chapter 10

Tash led them through big echoey rooms smelling of furniture polish and old wood. Every corner and table held a weird-looking machine. Some were all wires and plastic — like an early computer. A few looked like smooth sculptures of wood and metal; others like primitive espresso machines. *Old Man Blake's inventions*, Elly thought, as she scurried to catch up with the others.

Mojo followed them, yapping in excitement. 'Shush, Mojo!' Tash whirled on the dog, suddenly stern. Mojo whined softly and Tash leant down to give his ears a rub. 'We have

to be quiet,' she explained. 'I'm not supposed to go in the attic. Mum wants me to sit still like a good little girl and watch TV all day or something. Actually, she doesn't really care what I do as long as I stay out of her way and out of trouble.' Tash shrugged.

Elly felt her stomach clench as she listened to Tash talking about her mother. Mum would never have treated her like that. She bit her lip. They ran up a big staircase to the first floor, a smaller one to the second, an even smaller one to the third, before finally climbing a narrow, twisting staircase up to the attic.

The door creaked open onto a dim, long room with a low ceiling. Elly followed Tash and Mojo inside. Sierra crept behind, hyperventilating down the back of Elly's neck.

'Spookyyyy...' hissed Sierra.

It was. Elly looked around. A skylight let in just enough light to make out a long rectangle of a room crammed full of junk. Cobwebs hung everywhere, draggled ones like dirty rags and fresh ones with the spiders still sitting in them.

'What is this stuff?' Sierra was poking at a weird-looking box perched on a rickety table. The box was open on three sides and full of mirrors, wire and lots of dust. The whole attic was strewn with strange objects of all sizes and shapes.

'Careful!' Tash pulled Sierra away from the table. 'That's one of Grandad's crazy inventions. Mum's petrified that I'll break one of them, although that's a joke since they don't work. No one even knows what most of them are supposed to do. This is what I wanted to show you.' She led the way to the far end of the attic where a big trunk sat beneath the

skylight. Tash knelt and lifted the lid. It gave a reluctant, eerie squeak and Sierra squealed.

'Shhhh!' said Tash.

Elly peered in. It smelt musty, and for a moment, she couldn't see anything. Then a column of sunlight shone through the skylight and the dust haze and into the trunk.

'Oh!' gasped Elly. She couldn't believe it. Was that really . . . ? She collapsed onto her knees, stunned.

Tash reached into the trunk and lifted out the photograph. It was old and faded, in a dingy plastic frame, but it was still clearly a snap of three girls aged around eleven or twelve, all three caught in mid-jump. One of the girls had blonde hair in a ponytail; the other was tall and slender, with long dark hair; and the third girl . . .

Tash pointed to the blonde girl. 'That's my mum. I didn't recognize her at first because she's smiling and Mum never smiles.'

'And . . . oh my godfathers, that's *mine*!' Sierra poked her finger at the tall, long-haired girl.

Elly just sat, staring at the third girl in the picture. The attic had been haunted after all—by her mother's ghost.

Tears streamed down Elly's face. She couldn't stop them.

'Elly?' Sierra was beside her, crouching down, putting a gentle arm round her shoulders.

Tash was still holding the photo. 'What's the matter, Elly?'

Elly put her hands over her eyes, made herself breathe slowly and deeply, and waited. Sierra shushed Tash when she started asking more questions; Tash pulled Mojo back when he tried to climb up Elly to lick her tears away.

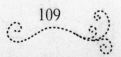

In a little while Elly found she could speak. 'Are there more?' Her voice was creaky. She swallowed and tried again. 'Other photos of them?'

'I don't know.' Tash's eyes looked worried, pale blue in the dusty light. She put the photo down. 'Hey, what's up, Elly? I figured the other girl must be your mum. She looks like you.'

'It is.'

It had to be said. Elly squished up her feelings and held them tight. 'She's dead. She died four months ago. She got breast cancer.'

She heard Tash gasp; saw her face change. Sierra's arm tightened around her and she saw that her friend's eyes were wet. 'I'm so sorry.'

Elly's heart was hammering. Suddenly she was scared. Scared that Sierra and Tash would stop thinking of her as their friend and start thinking of

her as the girl with the
mum that died. Like
everyone at school. She
didn't think she could bear
it if they started treating her differently . . .
carefully . . . or like some sort of freak.

'That's horrible, Elly. I'm really sorry.' Tash
was looking her right in the eyes, the same
old Tash as ever. Elly felt a rush of relief. It
was going to be OK. 'What about your dad?'
Tash continued in her no-nonsense way. 'Are
you guys close?'

Elly thought of her dad, of his blue eyes
that were all crinkly at the corners, his deep
laugh, his whiskery face whenever he tried to
grow stubble like her mum's actory friends.
There hadn't been much laughter since
Mum died, but there had been lots and lots
of hugging and just being together. He would
be missing her.

'Yes,' she said.

Tash smiled at her. 'That's good,' she said.

111

'And you've got us now, too.'

'That's right!' Sierra gave her another hug. 'We're gonna have the greatest summer ever. I'm so lucky to have met you guys. But it isn't luck, is it? We were meant to find each other. Our mums were friends. We've got the proof: the photo and the charms.'

'Maybe there are more photos in here.' Tash turned back to the trunk and began pulling things out and dumping them on the floor: old books, a tin full of buttons, a bunch of heavy old-fashioned keys, a porcelain door knob, a pair of ancient women's shoes with buttons instead of laces, a tarnished silver mirror, a moth-eaten teddy bear. And some old photograph albums. But they were full of black and white photos, taken long before their mothers had been born.

'No luck,' Tash sighed.

'There's nothing here but junk.'

Elly picked up the photo of the three girls. They looked so happy, her mother and her two friends, caught in time.

And then she saw it: 'She's wearing the necklace. Look!' Elly pointed to the pendant, a faint silver shape attached by an invisible chain to her mother's neck, floating in mid-air like the girls themselves.

'And there's my charm bracelet!'

'And my badge!'

'They're wearing our charms.' Elly shivered. It was odd seeing her pendant there in the photo: another time, another girl.

'They must have stopped being friends.' Sierra's voice was sad.

'That won't happen to us!' Tash sounded fierce. 'Here!' She dug the peace symbol from her pocket and clicked it apart so it fell into three pieces. She handed over the pendant and bracelet. 'Put them on. We gotta swear, right now, to always stay friends. No matter what!'

Elly felt her eyes sting. She blinked the hotness away. 'I swear!'

'And me!' cried Sierra. 'Cross my heart and hope to be pickled in cucumber juice if I ever break that promise.'

Elly slid her mother's necklace over her head. Sierra fastened the bracelet around her wrist. Tash had already pinned the badge on her T–shirt.

'Friends for ever!' they said together.

Chapter 11

Mojo scampered around the girls. Tash calmed him down while Elly helped Sierra gather the junk that needed to go back into the trunk.

Sierra dropped the tin of buttons into the trunk with a loud clank. She winced. 'Sorry!'

'Wait.' Elly knelt beside the trunk and peered inside. 'That thud didn't sound right.'

'What?' Sierra tucked her hair behind her ears.

Tash put Mojo down and joined them beside the trunk. 'It sounded echoey. I wonder . . .' She lifted out the button tin, then knocked

on the bottom of the trunk with her knuckles. The noise echoed like a drum. 'See? This trunk has a false bottom.'

'Yikes!' Sierra gave a squeal. Elly and Tash scrabbled around the bottom of the trunk, feeling for a catch or handle.

'Got it!' cried Elly. Her fingers closed around a leather strap slotted into the side of the trunk. She tugged. 'Here it comes!' The bottom stuck, then slid reluctantly up and out. Tash grabbed the other end and they lifted it out.

Only one thing sat in the secret compartment: a small cardboard box.

Tash gave them an excited look, then reached in and lifted out the box. She fumbled off the lid with nervous fingers. The sunlight had grown stronger all the time they had been in the attic, and Elly could

clearly see a small pile of
photographs lying in the
box. The image on the top
photograph showed the girls again.

'Spread them out here so we can look.'
Sierra patted the top of the trunk. Tash placed
the four photographs face up.

'Now that's weird,' Sierra said.

Elly had to agree. Whatever she had been
expecting, it wasn't this. Their mothers looked
the same age as in the first photo—and they
looked happy. But otherwise, the pictures
were . . . odd. In each photo, the girls had
struck a funny pose, joining together into a
human semaphore, arms and legs at strange
angles. 'They're just fooling around for the
camera,' Elly said.

'But why hide them in the bottom of the
trunk?' Tash shook her head. 'These photos
mean something, I know it.'

Sierra had turned over one of the photos.
'There's something written on the back: "Our

treasure!" Oh my godfathers!' She stared at them, her mouth open. 'Our mums must have found some sort of treasure on the island— diamonds maybe! Jewelled tiaras!—and these pictures are clues to where they hid it!'

Elly tried to keep calm as she examined the remaining pictures. 'It says the same thing on all of them! That's got to mean something. And look, the background's different in every photograph.'

'Dump everything back in the trunk and let's go to my bedroom,' said Tash. 'We need better light and a map.'

In ten minutes they were all sitting around the desk in Tash's large bedroom, staring at the photographs while Tash marked locations on a map of the island.

'That's the north side of the lake by the caravan park,' Sierra said, pointing to the first photo. Tash put a big fat dot on the map to correspond. 'One down. This one's easy too—that's the "Welcome to Sunday Island" sign as you drive off the causeway.' She placed another dot on the map. 'But the last two are harder. Wait . . . I know that one!' She picked up a photo with a wooden building in the background. 'That's the old barn by the stables here. It's a bit more run down now, but I'm sure that's it.' Another dot went onto the map.

'This last one has a coastline in the background,' Elly mused. 'I don't know where that is.'

'Me neither.' Sierra frowned at the picture.

'Let me look.' Tash picked up the photo and studied it. 'Those rocks. See those, just on the edge of the picture? That's Dead Man's Point. Got it!' And the last dot was scribbled onto the map.

'OK,' Elly said, after staring at the map with

the four places marked for several minutes. 'What does it mean? Maybe they were just messing around.'

'Oh, don't wreck my dreams of wealth and luxury,' moaned Sierra. 'Here,' she got up from the desk and struck a pose from one of the photos. 'Come on, girls, let's copy the pictures—maybe it'll give us inspiration.'

Elly and Sierra pulled Tash into the middle of the room. She protested: 'This is silly.'

'Silly is good,' Sierra admonished. 'It's magic: you have to be silly at least fifteen times every day or you turn into one of those old boring pieces of fudge called a grown-up. Come on!'

It was like playing Twister. After a few minutes, they collapsed in a giggling heap on the floor. 'Well, that was fun, but I still don't get it.' Sierra sighed and stared at the ceiling.

'Unless . . .' With a squeal of excitement, she leapt to her feet and dashed to the desk. 'Where's that pencil? Have you got a ruler? Great! Let's play connect the dots!'

She drew a line from each of the spots to the others. The result looked like a giant kite shape with two lines intersecting in the middle. 'Aha!' Sierra crowed. 'X really does mark the spot. That's where the treasure is!'

''Fraid not.' Tash sounded glum. 'There isn't any buried treasure there.'

'There has to be!'

'No. That part of the island sits on solid granite.'

'Noooo!' Sierra collapsed onto the floor. She lay on her back and spread her arms and legs out into an X shape. 'And I was so sure X marked the spot.' Her voice was deeply dramatic, and Elly couldn't help giggling as she watched Sierra stare tragically at the ceiling.

And then Elly realized what she was looking at. 'Sierra, you're a genius!'

'What?' Sierra jerked upright, staring at her.

'No! Lie back down. Make the X.'

Sierra rolled her eyes but stretched out on the floor again.

'Look, Tash. Do you see it?'

Tash frowned at Sierra for a moment, glanced at the photos and her eyes grew wide.

'You've both gone bonkers,' Sierra said, jumping up and joining them at the desk.

'I knew it!' Elly said. 'We've been looking at the wrong thing. It isn't the locations that are important, it's the poses. They're making letters!'

'Human alphabet soup?' Sierra squinted at the pictures but, once pointed out, it was obvious.

'O H O K,' Tash read out. 'Um . . .'

'Oh, OK?' suggested Elly.

'That still doesn't make any sense,' Sierra said. 'Is there any place on the island that's called Ohok?'

Tash shook her head. 'They can't be in the right order. But look, if you switch the first two around it spells—'

'HOOK!' Elly and Sierra shouted together.

'Is there anywhere on Sunday Island that's called "Hook", or that has a "hook" in it?' Elly asked.

Tash shook her head. 'No, sorry.'

'But it *must* mean something!' Elly wasn't going to give up now. It felt as though her mother was sending her a message. 'Let me have another look at the map.'

Elly twisted it that way and this, studying the island. 'Look. Just there.' She pointed to Mirror Cove. 'If you turn the map this way, that bunch of rocks there looks just like a

hook. What do you think?'

Tash opened her mouth to say something, but before she could speak there was a call from downstairs.

'Miss Natasha? Your mother is home.'

'Who's that?' Sierra asked.

'That's Jasper,' Tash replied. 'He's like, well, he takes care of us.'

'Like a butler? Cool!' Sierra squealed. 'You are proper posh.'

Elly noticed that Tash's expression had changed. All the sparkle and sturdiness seemed to have faded away. 'What's wrong?' Elly asked.

'She's back.' Tash bit off the words. 'Mum has been away on business. I didn't think she was coming home today. I am going to be in big trouble.'

Chapter 12

'I've got to get cleaned up,' Tash muttered, inspecting her grimy shorts and T–shirt. 'Could you guys find some clean and boring clothes, *please*?' She darted through a door and Elly heard gushing taps and the sound of frantic scrubbing.

Sierra shrugged and walked over to investigate the wardrobe. 'Clean and boring coming up.' The bathroom noises were joined by the clattering of hangers and faint grunts of disapproval.

When Tash emerged, Elly's mouth fell open. Her friend's spiky hair had disappeared.

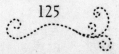

Tash had a soft, shiny blonde bob that just covered her ears. She looked like some normal, tame girl.

Sierra pointed to a crisp white shirt and tailored khaki shorts lying on the bed. 'Classics,' she said. 'Your mum will love them.'

In a moment, the new Tash was dressed.

'Whoa, Tash, looking good.' Sierra cocked her head as she studied the effect. 'But, d'you know, I prefer the old Tash.'

'Me too,' said Elly.

Tash shrugged. 'My mother won't stay long. She never does.' She started out of the door.

'Wait!' cried Elly. 'We swore, remember? You can't go without this.' She held out Tash's badge with the silver charm.

Tash gave a brief smile and pinned it onto her shirt. 'Thanks! Both of you. See you guys later.'

'That's what you think,' Elly

said. 'We're coming
with you.'

A tall man with faded ginger hair waited at
the bottom of the stairs. He was wearing a
dark suit and looked worried, but he cheered
up when he saw Tash.

'Where is she, Jasper?' Tash asked.

'In her office, Miss Natasha. And may I say
I'm pleased to see you looking rather more
tidy than usual. She'll be anxious to see you.'

'I doubt it.' Tash motioned Elly and Sierra
to follow.

As their footsteps clumped over polished
floorboards and sighed across deep Chinese
and Persian rugs, Elly realized she was
nervous about meeting Tash's mother. If her
own daughter was scared of her ... Stop being
silly, she told herself. After all, this woman
had been one of her mother's closest friends.
She couldn't be that bad.

But when she followed Tash into a cold,

neat room, and met the eyes of the woman seated at the desk, she knew she was wrong. Tash's mum *was* that bad.

'Hello, Mother.' Tash walked slowly forward, leant down and pecked her mother's cheek. 'I've brought some friends of mine to meet you.'

'Natasha, darling.' Tash's mother stood up and gave her daughter a quick hug before stepping back and looking her up and down. She was a short, thin woman wearing a tailored trouser suit and blunt-cut blonde hair.

'You've grown again!' Mrs Blake-Reynolds continued. 'And how nice to see you wearing something clean for once. But where on earth  did you find those ghastly purple flip-flops?' She glanced at Sierra and Elly. 'Lovely to meet you, girls. Are you visiting the island for the summer?' Without

waiting for an answer, she turned back to Tash. 'What's kept you, darling? I arrived nearly . . .' She paused, and her lips folded into a grim line. 'Where did you find that?' Tash's mother pointed at the badge pinned to her daughter's shirt. 'You've been in the attic again, haven't you?'

Uh-oh. Elly's stomach writhed. Her fault! She'd made Tash pin the charm to her shirt.

'Yes.' Tash put a protective hand over the pin. 'I found it in the attic. But it's amazing! Guess what—'

'I'm sorry,' Mrs Blake-Reynolds interrupted, turning to Elly and Sierra. 'I think it's time for you girls to go. I'm sorry to cut your visit short, but I need to speak privately to Natasha.'

'Mum! You can't just send them away! Don't you see who they look like? They're your friends' daughters: your friends from those photographs in the trunk. They had their mother's charms—that's why I went looking for yours.'

Elly had never seen someone's face go properly white before, like in books. For a moment Tash's mum looked as if she might faint. Then she just looked angry. Elly had a horrid moment where she thought Mrs Blake-Reynolds might shout at them. Instead she drew herself up very stiff and straight and said: 'I must ask you girls to leave at once.' She leant over her desk and picked up a phone. 'Jasper, please come to my office and escort the young ladies out.'

'Don't bother!' Sierra looked ready to spit with fury like a cat. 'Bye, Tash!' She gave the  stunned Tash a cheery wave, turned on her heels and, head high, marched out of the room. 'Come on, Elly.'

Elly caught Mrs Blake-Reynolds's eye. Her own face

must have shown what she was feeling, because Tash's mother opened her mouth and Elly thought for a second she was going to apologize and say it was all a mistake. But then she shut her mouth again. Elly turned and followed Sierra.

That evening, Elly and Sierra sat in Sierra's dad's caravan in the tiny living area, watching TV. Aunt Dina had let Elly stay over, 'as long as you get to bed at a decent hour'. Elly had every intention of following her aunt's orders and turning in early—before dawn anyway.

'What an evil woman!' said Sierra. She looked down at her feet in the pink flip-flops. 'I just feel so sorry for Tash, having to put up with that.'

Elly was about to reply when an eerie howl echoed through the caravan park.

'That's Mojo!'

'Quick!' Sierra jumped to open the door. 'Before he wakes my dad. And everyone else.'

They whistled and called, and the dog came scampering up at once.

'There's a note!' Elly grabbed Mojo's collar while Sierra knelt to retrieve the paper. She carried it back into the light. Elly watched the little dog trot off, his job done, then shut the door and joined her. 'Well?'

'Tash is waiting at the tree house.' Sierra looked up at Elly. 'She wants us to come.'

'Now?' Elly felt her stomach tense.

'Look at this.' Sierra held out the paper. 'No drawings or decorations. It doesn't say "Super Secret Message" or anything.' She frowned. 'Something's definitely wrong.'

The journey was slow: thick clouds covered the moon and stars completely. If they hadn't had a torch, Elly knew they wouldn't have been able to see a metre  in front of them. They headed into a surprisingly strong wind. Even over the wind, Elly could hear Sierra muttering about having to climb the rope ladder again.

The wind was blowing their hair straight back from their faces by the time they reached the towering black bulk of the maze. Elly's ears were freezing. They headed into the maze. It shouldn't have been so scary this time, but the sound of the wind rattling and whining overhead made Elly's heart thud. At least this time they knew the route. It only took a few minutes to reach the centre and the giant tree. The windows of the tree house glimmered with a faint light.

'She's there!' Elly felt a surge of relief. Sierra must have been just as eager to get out of the dark and wind because she scampered up the rope ladder like a squirrel. The tree house door swung open at once and Tash waved them inside.

Half a dozen candles flickered as the wind found its way through cracks in the walls. Elly shivered.

'Sorry, I didn't have time to organize anything fun. I had a tough time sneaking out with Mum home.' Tash's voice was mournful. She motioned to them to huddle near her on the pile of cushions. Her hair was still in the shiny, neat bob.

'How long is she staying?' Sierra asked.

'I don't know.' Tash sighed. 'Weeks, it sounds like. But there's worse news.'

There was a pause. Elly looked at Sierra, then Tash. No one seemed to want to speak.

'Don't make us beg. Spill!' Sierra said at last.

'I-It's my mum.' Even in the dim light, Elly could see Tash starting to blush. 'She doesn't want me to hang out with you guys any more.'

'What?' Sierra's voice was dangerously quiet.

'Why not?' Elly asked. 'What did we do?'

'I'm not sure you'll want me to tell you.' Tash's voice sounded flat and tired.

'Come on,' Sierra said. 'We have a right to know.'

A huge gust of wind tore across the maze and shook the entire tree. The tree house rocked, and Elly screamed as the candles blew out. So did Sierra and Tash. Then there was just the sound of Mojo, whimpering in the darkness. Elly sat, stunned, waiting for what she knew was coming. And it happened: with a huge crack of thunder and a flash of lightning that seemed right over their heads, the skies split apart and rain hammered down. After a few more moments of scared silence, Elly heard Tash rustling about in her pockets. A match flared and Tash scooted around the tree house on hands and knees, re-lighting

the candles. 'That was a sign if ever I saw one.'
She gave a shaky laugh.

'Don't be silly!' Sierra snapped. 'It's only
the weather. It's got nothing to do with any of
this mess.'

'What did your mother say? You have to
tell us,' Elly said. She had to know, even
though her stomach seemed crammed full
of butterflies. 'It's something to do with their
friendship, isn't it? Our mums.'

Elly's heart sank further as Tash looked up
at her and nodded.

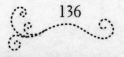

Chapter 13

'It started their second summer together on the island.' Tash's voice floated over the steady drumming of rain. In the flickering candlelight, her face looked oddly pale. Sierra sat cross-legged a little further away, leaning her head forward so that her face was hidden behind a curtain of hair. Mojo crouched near Tash, peering anxiously in turn at all of them.

'They wanted to do something to celebrate their friendship,' Tash said. 'They made a time capsule and buried it, somewhere where only the three of them could ever find it. Most of the things they put in weren't worth much,

but my mum added one of the Blake family heirlooms—a ruby brooch.'

'Buried treasure all along,' Sierra murmured.

'They stayed friends,' Tash continued. 'The summer they all turned eighteen they had a reunion on the island. They went to dig up the treasure and . . .'

Elly's gut clenched. She knew what was coming.

'. . . it was gone. That was the end. They never spoke again.'

There was a long silence in the flickering candlelight. Mojo whimpered. Elly stared into space as the meaning sank into her brain. She turned to Tash.

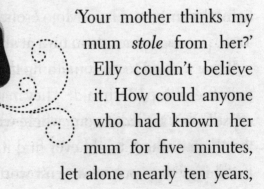

'Your mother thinks my mum *stole* from her?' Elly couldn't believe it. How could anyone who had known her mum for five minutes, let alone nearly ten years,

think that she would
be capable of such
a thing?

'One of them did,' Tash said.
'I don't know if it was your mum or Sierra's.
Does it matter? It wasn't you guys who did it.
It doesn't have anything to do with us.'

Tash sounded desperate, but Elly was too
angry to care. 'My mum was not a thief!'

'I don't like it either but my mum would
hardly steal her own jewellery. And she
wouldn't be so upset about it if she had,
would she?'

Elly just stared at her. How could Tash even
think like this?

'My mum may be ditsy . . .' Sierra spoke at
last, her voice was growing louder with every
syllable. '. . . but she is *not* a thief! And *your*
mum—'

'OK. What?' Tash was nearly shouting now
too. 'What about my mum?'

'She's the one who's causing all the

139

problems! It's only her word against theirs. She acts like she owns the island and accuses our mums of stealing stuff!'

'She *does* own the island.'

'Yeah? Well, she doesn't have to be so mean, does she?' Sierra jumped to her feet. She stood with her hands on her hips, glaring down at Tash, who slowly stood up.

'I think your mum made the whole thing up,' Sierra continued. 'She's a control freak and she doesn't like her little darling associating with the likes of us.'

'That's crazy!' Tash shouted.

'This whole thing is crazy,' muttered Elly. She felt sick. It was all happening again — just like it had to their mothers. A jinx, a curse. Whatever. She needed to get out of here. 'I'm going now. Are you coming, Sierra?'

'You bet.' Sierra ran her hands through her

hair, bangles clattering.
She looked about to burst
into tears.

Mojo was whining. He
scrabbled at Tash's legs and she
bent to pick him up. 'Go on then,' she said.
'We swore we'd be friends for ever. I guess you
didn't mean it.'

'You've got to decide who to believe,' Sierra
said. 'Who's it gonna be, Tash? Your friends
or your mother?'

There was no answer.

As Elly shut the door behind them, she
caught a last glimpse of Tash, standing quite
still in the empty tree house, her face hidden
in Mojo's fur.

'Don't make a hasty decision you'll end up
regretting, El.' It was the morning after the
storm, and Aunt Dina was pouring a cup
of hot chocolate for Elly. She set it on the
kitchen table. 'Drink up. Chocolate is the

best medicine I know for heartache.' She placed a loving hand on Elly's head before sitting down with her own cup.

'I'm not going to change my mind. I want to go home.' Elly had thumped her bags downstairs at 8 a.m. She'd come home after the meeting at Tash's, woken at dawn, and spent the early morning packing.

'I wish you'd tell me what all this is about.' Her aunt was frowning with worry. 'Friends are bound to fall out from time to time; you just have to work through it.'

'This isn't like that.' It hurt too much to talk about, even to Aunt Dina. Finding the silver pendant and everything that had happened afterwards—meeting Sierra and Tash, solving the mystery of the charms and discovering that their mothers had been friends before them—had felt like a gift from her mother. Last night in the tree house had destroyed all that. The friendship was broken, like the peace symbol. It felt as though she had lost her mother for a second time. Now she just wanted to leave the island. She looked down at her green flip-flops and sighed.

'Get that inside you.' Her aunt set a plate of bacon, eggs, sausage, fried mushrooms and tomatoes in front of her. 'You probably won't get a decent meal the rest of the day. I'll drive you to the mainland and put you on a train. Nick can pick you up at the railway station. If that's what you really want.'

'It is. But do I have time to go to the caravan park and say goodbye to Sierra before we go?'

'Just about. Eat up and pop along. Be quick or you'll miss the tide and we'll have to wait till this afternoon.'

When Elly knocked on the caravan door it

143

was answered by Sierra's father. He was still in his dressing gown and looked rumpled and upset.

'*Excelente!*' he cried, holding the door open for her. 'Come in and convince that crazy daughter of mine to stay. In there!' He pointed to Sierra's bedroom. 'Go on. Talk her out of it.'

Sierra's bedroom looked like the aftermath of a hurricane. Clothes, jewellery, magazines and shoes were strewn everywhere. In the middle of the mess were a suitcase, a duffel bag and Sierra, stuffing clothes into the bag as quickly as her arms could stuff. She saw Elly and jumped to her feet.

'Good! I wanted to say goodbye.'

'That's what I've come to do.'

Sierra blinked. 'You're leaving too?'

Elly nodded, too miserable to

144

chance speaking.

'Well, actually, I'm glad. I felt rubbish about bailing on you and running for home. But . . . ' she turned in the direction of the main room and shouted: 'I don't want to stay where I'm not wanted!'

'*Princesa!*' Sierra's dad stuck his head into the room. 'Of course I want you. I'm just not used to having anyone around. Give me another chance, *por favor!*'

'Sorry.' Sierra shook her head. 'All out of fresh chances.' She turned to Elly, who felt herself blushing with embarrassment. 'Can your aunt give me a ride to the mainland? I've rung my mum. She's expecting me.'

'Ah, *maldita sea!* Suit yourself!' Mr Cruz ducked out of sight and Elly heard him stamp out of the caravan.

Sierra shrugged. 'I get my temper from him.' She sighed. 'Now help me pack and let's get out of here.'

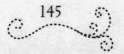

The morning had been clear, but it was starting to drizzle as Elly and Sierra made their way to Aunt Dina's cottage. Sierra carried her handbag and dragged the overstuffed duffel, and Elly struggled with the heaviest suitcase she'd ever lifted. 'You'll never manage these on the train!'

'You'll be there to help now.' Sierra shook damp hair out of her eyes. 'It's great you're going back too. We can get together in London. The summer will be OK.'

Elly nodded. It would be great to keep in touch with Sierra, but the summer would never be OK, not as long as Tash thought her mother was a thief and, worse, a bad friend.

 She noticed that Sierra was still wearing her pink flip-flops, just like she was still wearing her green ones.

They turned the corner into her aunt's street. There,

parked as usual in front of the cottage, but with Aunt Dina bent over the engine, was her aunt's ancient VW Beetle. It was bright orange and thoroughly temperamental.

'Oh no,' groaned Elly. She dumped the suitcase beside the car.

Sierra tugged the duffel the last few metres and collapsed on it in a panting heap. 'Are we meant to be going in . . . that? Wow.'

Aunt Dina emerged from around the side of the car, her hands smeared with oil. 'The Bug's just having a bit of a wobble. Hi, Sierra. What's with the luggage?'

'She wants to go home too. Can you put us both on the train?'

'Do your parents know?' Aunt Dina looked taken aback.

'Yes, I've phoned Mum. And Dad knows. I'd really appreciate a lift, Miss Valentine.'

Elly's aunt wiped her hands on a piece

of rag. 'Well . . . if you're certain. Pop your luggage in with Elly's. Hurry, now. We've only got fifteen minutes to beat the tide.'

They managed to squeeze the duffel into the boot, but they had to cram Sierra and her suitcase in the back seat. Elly held her breath as she watched her aunt turn the ignition switch. The engine cranked, stalled, cranked again and caught. The old car spluttered and chugged into life.

'Atta' Bug!' Aunt Dina said. 'She's never let me down yet. Well, not for long.' At that moment, the sky went dark and the drizzle turned into a thunderstorm.

Rain hammered on the roof of the VW. Aunt Dina flicked on the windscreen wipers. 'This looks like one of our freak summer storms. We'd best get you off the island before the causeway floods.' She

clunked into first gear,
but just as they began to
roll away from the kerb a
figure loomed out of the storm
and began to pound on Aunt Dina's window.

Chapter 14

'Oh my godfathers,' Sierra cried. 'It's *her*!'

Tash's mum, totally drenched, pulled open the car door. She was holding her mobile in one hand and looked frantic. Elly got a funny feeling in her stomach.

'I can't find her!' Mrs Blake-Reynolds shouted over the noise of the storm. Her eyes were wide with panic. 'I can't get through on my phone—no reception. Tash has run away! We can't find her anywhere. Do you girls know where she is? Please!' She burst into tears.

'She'll be fine.' Aunt Dina climbed out of

the Bug and put an arm round Mrs Blake-Reynolds's shoulders. 'Getting into a state won't help. Girls, do you have any ideas?'

Elly felt awful. Tash must be really upset to have run away. But where would she go?

And then she knew.

'I think I know where Tash has gone.'

'*Where?*' Aunt Dina and Tash's mum asked at the same time.

'Mirror Cove. We found clues about a time capsule our mothers made years ago. I think Tash has gone to the cove to find it.'

'Yes!' Sierra cried. 'That's got to be it.'

Mrs Blake-Reynolds shook her head. 'We did bury the capsule in a cave at Mirror Cove.

 But it's not there any more. It was . . . ' She glanced at Elly and Sierra and her voice trailed away. 'What matters is that Tash might be there,' Aunt Dina said.

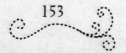

'Come inside, Mrs Blake-Reynolds, and we'll phone the police. If she's out in this storm, we need to find her. And you need to change out of those wet clothes before you catch your death.'

Elly watched her aunt shepherd Tash's mum inside. She knew what she had to do.

'I'm going to Mirror Cove. I can't just stay here if Tash is in trouble.'

Sierra nodded. 'I'm coming with you.'

Elly darted inside the cottage and grabbed a pair of waterproofs without being spotted. Aunt Dina's anorak was massively too big for Sierra and flapped like a wet sheet in the wind once they were outside. Elly would not have thought it possible, but it began to rain even harder. She shrugged and began to run in the direction of Mirror Cove, Sierra hard on her heels.

Elly was glad she had her waterproof as she powered up the hill. It was a long wet slog of a run. The peaty paths were slippery underfoot. She and Sierra took more than one tumble on the narrow footpath to Mirror Cove. They would be sore and bruised tomorrow, but that was the least of her worries.

She kept seeing that last glimpse of Tash in the tree house: holding Mojo and crying into his fur. No matter how angry they had been, she and Sierra should have seen the truth: Tash needed them. Elly's mum had been the best mum in the world while she was alive, and she still had a dad and an aunt who loved her to pieces. But Tash didn't seem to have anyone except Mojo. She had counted on her friends and they had let her down. Elly ran faster.

They were sliding and slipping down the path through the beech wood when a brown, furry shape darted out from the trees and leapt straight at them. Elly screamed and tripped over. Sierra piled into her with a very unladylike word.

'Woof!' said the animal. Mojo! It was as if Elly's thoughts had conjured him up. He barked again, then began whining.

'That proves Tash must be nearby,' panted Sierra. 'Let's keep going.'

'Good Boy, Mojo!' Elly said, giving him a quick pat on the head.

'Come on,' Sierra said. 'We need to hurry.'

She was right. Elly felt it too. They had to find Tash quickly.

A few minutes later they were standing above Mirror Cove. Elly glanced at Sierra. Her friend's face was set and determined. Sierra didn't hesitate. She eased over the cliff edge and scooted down the hill on her bottom, even though she was in her best jeans. When she reached the two-metre drop, she lowered herself by her hands as though she did it every day.

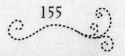

Elly followed down the slippery, nearly vertical path. Mojo seemed determined to trip her up. At the drop he stopped and whined anxiously at her, his eyes pleading.

'Oh, all right!' Elly scooped him up in one arm and edged down, supporting herself with her free hand. She jumped and fell onto her knees with a painful thump. 'Ow!'

Mojo wriggled out of her arms and scampered away, barking at the top of his lungs. 'That's gratitude!' she groaned as she climbed to her feet. But in a few seconds she'd reached the beach, where Sierra stood peering through the rain.

'No sign of her!' Sierra sounded as though she was about to burst into tears.

Elly scanned the beach and cliff face. Nothing. Had she been wrong? Maybe Tash hadn't come here after all.

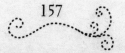

But then . . .

'Woof! Woof! Woof!'

Mojo was standing on a rocky ledge, barking at the waves crashing directly below him.

'There's something in the water.' Sierra's voice fell to a husky whisper.

Elly felt giddy. She ran towards the dog, who stood barking at the sea. With every step, she became more certain of what it was that floated on the waves.

Tash's scarf. The green and purple one she'd been wearing the first time they met her. It surged to and fro in the waves like a frond of seaweed. Elly couldn't move. She thought she might throw up. Then she noticed Sierra beside her, pulling off her waterproof, kicking off her flip-flops.

'*What are you doing?!*'

'I'm going in.' Sierra shoved her charm bracelet and bangles into a pocket of the waterproof and anchored it with a rock.

'You can't!' Elly said, grabbing Sierra's arm. 'It's too dangerous. We should go and get help.'

'That would take too long.' Sierra twisted free. 'We've got to do something.' She started towards the water, then turned back to give Elly a quick hug. 'Don't worry. I'm a strong swimmer. I'll be back in a minute.'

Elly watched Sierra slip off the rocks into the water, still wearing her clothes. She struck out towards the scarf. In a few strokes, she'd reached it. She trod water for a moment. Then, to Elly's horror, she dived under water and disappeared.

'Come back, Sierra! Oh, please . . . come back!'

Thirty seconds by her watch. A minute. Ninety seconds. Panic welled up. Something had gone wrong! Two minutes! No one could hold their breath that long! Oh

God! What should she do? Elly scraped off her waterproof, kicked off her flip-flops,  and plunged into the sea after her friends, her heart thudding with terror. What choice did she have?

She made herself concentrate on getting to the scarf as quickly as possible, but it was harder than she had expected—her clothes seemed to drag her down, the sea was rough and she was buffeted by the waves. She was shaking with fear and cold when she finally reached it.

The scarf floated on the waves. Still in the same place. That was odd. The waves were getting bigger, rougher. The storm was making the sea angry.

Elly gulped a lungful of air and dived beneath the surface. But the waters were so churned up she could only see greyish murk. She surfaced and gasped for air. She shook the salt water out of her eyes and looked again for the scarf. There!

She reached for it, but the waves batted it out of her hand. Treading water was hard and she'd never been good at it. The run had tired her; now she was getting dangerously exhausted—her legs and arms felt heavy. The waves crashed onto the cliff face, and Elly realized she was being pulled slowly but surely towards the rocks. The waves would smash her on them. And that would be the end.

She gathered the last of her strength and lunged for the scarf again. This time her hand closed round it. She grabbed it with  both hands, kicked hard with her feet, and tugged. And again. It was attached to something under the water! That was why it stayed in one place. She

gave another tug, to make sure.

The scarf tugged back.

Had she imagined that? Had the waves done it? No: there it was again—two strong tugs. That wasn't the sea—it was Sierra! She was down there somewhere.

Elly knew what she had to do next, but she had never been so scared in her life. *Just do it!* She filled her lungs again and dived deep below the churning waves, pulling herself along the scarf hand over hand. It was hard work, like swimming through treacle. She kicked frantically, trying to speed up. Her lungs were burning. Should she let go? Go back up for air? For some crazy reason, she kept going. Even though she wasn't going to make it. Her lungs felt as if they were on fire, and stars were starting to explode like fireworks behind her eyes. It was too late now . . .

And then she felt herself being pulled along. Somehow, she kept her mouth shut, fighting the desperate need to breathe. Now she was moving upwards, reeled in like a fish. And then … Splash! Her head burst out of the water into air.

Elly clung to the scarf, gulping and coughing. There was just enough dim light filtering from high overhead to make out a small cavern surrounding her. She was in a sort of pond in the middle of the cave, and two figures stood on the shore, pulling her in by the scarf. Sierra *and* Tash!

In a moment, they had her out of the water and she was in the middle of the best group hug of her life.

Chapter 15

Elly was laughing and crying at the same time. 'I thought you'd both drowned!' she said. They looked funny in their soaking wet clothes.

'It's all my fault.' Tash shook her head. 'I couldn't stop thinking about what you'd said about your mums. I knew you were right. The only thing that made sense was that the treasure was still here somewhere. I decided to find it.

'When I got here this morning the sea was calm and I saw the top of the tunnel that leads in here. So I left my scarf as a marker and dived in.'

'Did you find the treasure?' Elly asked.

'Not yet. But I'm sure it's here.'

'We can help now,' Sierra said. 'I don't think it's safe to swim back through the tunnel with that storm going on.'

'Well,' Tash said, 'let's spread out. If you see anything, shout. I brought a waterproof torch.' She flicked on the torch and swept the beam of light around the cavern.

The girls set out in different directions, searching for a clue as to where the treasure was buried. Over the centuries, water had worn away the cavern floor. It was smooth and cool beneath Elly's bare feet as she walked away from the pool that hid the underwater tunnel. This part of the cave was darker. The floor sloped sharply uphill. She must be well above sea-level now, perhaps under the cliff itself.

Elly hesitated. The cave's

ceiling had grown lower and lower. Now it was only centimetres overhead. She didn't like thinking about all that rock above her, but she couldn't give up now: she had reached the back of the cave. She strained her eyes in the dim light, studying the stone wall blocking her path. Nothing. And nowhere to go from here. Elly's heart sank. Maybe Sierra or Tash were having better luck.

As she turned to go, Elly's hand brushed against an irregularity in the wall. She knelt to get a better look. Were those lines carved into the stone? 'Tash!' she shouted, her heart banging with hope. 'Bring your torch.'

In a moment the girls were beside her and a beam of white light played over the cliff wall. 'There, look!' Elly pointed. 'It's a peace symbol!'

'*Whooop!*' Sierra's scream echoed round the cave.

'We've found it,' Tash breathed. She tucked the torch away and began digging at the rocks piled beneath the symbol. It looked as if there had been a rock fall here years ago. Elly and Sierra joined in. For some minutes there was only the sound of scrabbling, clunking and puffing as the girls shifted rocks and rubble.

'There's a hole here!' Tash said, her voice more tense than ever. 'Right at the base of the wall.' She knelt down and cleared the last of the dirt from the hole. 'No! It's empty!'

'Let me see. Maybe we haven't reached the bottom.' Elly knelt down for a closer look. The bottom of the hole was all loosely packed stones. It would take a pickaxe to clear them. Their mothers couldn't have dug any deeper. Slowly, she climbed to her feet.

'That's it, then.' Sierra sounded as miserable as Elly felt. 'This has to be the place. And the treasure's just not here.'

'I don't care,' Elly said. '*None* of our mothers stole it. There has to be another explanation.' She jumped into the hole and stamped in frustration. Suddenly one foot broke through the rubble and she sank up to her knee. It felt as though there was nothing but empty air beneath her! She tried to pull her leg out of the hole, but as she did she felt the ground beneath her shift. Elly screamed as the bottom of the hole crumbled in a shower of stone and she dropped into nothingness.

She hit solid ground with a thud that knocked the air out of her. She lay curled up, gasping for breath as mud and sand showered down.

'Elly! Are you all right?' Sierra was screaming from somewhere overhead. Elly groaned and rolled up onto hands and knees. First Tash, then Sierra, jumped down to land beside her.

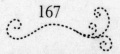

Tash put an arm round her shoulders. 'Are you hurt?'

'Not really. Just surprised.' Elly stood up with a groan.

Tash flicked on her torch and shone it around. 'It's part of a tunnel, look!'

They were standing in a massive hole, over a metre high and wide. Either end was a mouth opening onto blackness. Then the torch shone on something on the ground beside them, and Elly didn't spare another thought about the discovery of one of the island's historic tunnels.

At some point, after their mothers had dug their small hole and buried their time  capsule, the treasure they had thought so safe had broken through and landed in this tunnel. Then more rock must have slipped down to make it look as if the treasure had been taken. It had been lying here all those years.

Elly knelt down and lifted the treasure—it was an old, rusty biscuit tin.

'Oh my godfathers!' Sierra cried. 'Is that what I think it is?'

'It must be!' Tash's voice wobbled.

They scrambled out of the collapsed tunnel and went to the driest, lightest part of the cave. Tash held the torch with a shaking hand while Sierra opened the tin. They took turns taking out the treasures one by one: a photo of their mothers, curling and spotted with damp despite being wrapped in cling film; a heavy gold brooch studded with red stones; a shared diary they posted back and forth with entries by all three girls while they were away at school; an old-fashioned cassette recorder tape, labelled 'Disco-Divas'.

Elly's fingers closed on a simple silver locket. She lifted it into the light and saw the initials

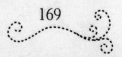

SEV. When she opened it, her mother's face smiled up at her. Elly felt tears begin to spill from her eyes. She felt her mother's love, as strongly as if she were right there in the cave with her. Elly sat, staring at the photograph, until a new noise made her glance up.

Sierra was sitting cross-legged, reading a letter and choking back sobs. When she noticed Elly watching, she sniffed loudly. 'It's a letter from my dad to my mother from when they first met. Ooo, it's so sweet. I guess they did love each other once.' She carefully folded the letter and put it with the other treasures.

Tash was also staring down at a piece of paper. 'I don't believe it!' she said.

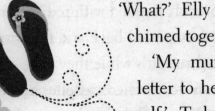

'What?' Elly and Sierra chimed together.

'My mum wrote a letter to her grown-up self,' Tash explained. 'She wanted to be a champion surfer when she

grew up. She was
going to travel the
world, fighting for
environmental causes. I
mean, I didn't even know my mum could
surf.' Tash looked stunned. 'She never—'

Whatever Tash was going to say was lost in
the rumble of a rockslide. Tash jumped and
dropped her torch. Elly heard it smash and
the light went out.

'Oh no!' moaned Sierra. Then: 'What's that
noise?'

Elly held her breath. She heard it: a
scrabbling, snuffling noise. Getting closer!

Sierra screamed.

A speck of light grew on the opposite side of
the cave. Right in the middle of it appeared a
familiar doggy face.

'Mojo!' Tash shrieked and leapt to her feet.
Mojo popped out of the hole and darted
across the cave to Tash, who gathered him in
her arms. He bore it for a few seconds, then

wriggled free and ran back to the hole, where he stopped and barked. It was obvious that he wanted them to follow.

'I vote we do what we're told.' Sierra scooped the treasures back into the tin and jumped to her feet. Tash was already inspecting the hole.

'It leads back to the beach,' she cried.

Mojo's tunnel was a tight squeeze, but it was only a couple of metres long. Tash went first, grunting and struggling. Halfway along she stuck until Elly and Sierra pushed her out. Sierra slipped through in no time, shoving the tin in front of her. Elly wriggled through last, fingers scrabbling, toes pushing. It was only slightly less horrible than the long underwater dive. She felt her hands being grabbed and Tash and Sierra pulled her free.

The storm was over and it was hot summer on Sunday Island once more.

Elly stood between Tash and Sierra, squinting through bright sunshine at the grown-ups rushing towards them.

Aunt Dina, Tash's mum and Sierra's dad swept down upon them. Elly just had time to smile at her friends before she was smothered in a duvet-like hug. When she was released at last, Elly saw that her aunt was struggling not to cry. There was a moment's awkward silence, then the grown-ups all started talking at once.

'What on earth were you thinking?' Tash's mum had switched from relieved to furious. 'Going into the cave during a storm! You've always been very sensible, but that was crazy and stupid. You could have been . . .' Her voice trailed off as she wrapped Tash in a fierce hug.

Now it was Aunt Dina's turn. 'And what did *you* mean by running off without a word? And as for going into that cave . . . we are going to have a nice long chat about island safety.'

Sierra's dad nodded agreement, but he kept hugging Sierra, his eyes brimming with tears.

'Can you be quiet for a minute, please?' Tash shouted over them.

Magically, the adults stopped talking.

'I'm sorry,' Tash said. 'Maybe I shouldn't have gone in the cave, but the storm hadn't started then. And you guys were in and out of that cave when you were our age, so you can't really talk. But I was looking for something important.' She handed the tin to her mother. 'We found the treasure.'

'But . . . how?' Mrs Blake-Reynolds stared at the rusty biscuit tin in her hands, her face blank with shock. 'It was there all along?'

Tash nodded. 'You dug your hole right on top of one of the old tunnels. The tin fell through. You should have kept digging.'

Tash's mum shook her head. Her face had gone still and sad.

She looked up and caught Elly's eye. 'I'm so very sorry to hear about your mother.' Tash's mum blinked back tears. 'Your aunt just told me. I had no idea. I . . . I loved Phee very much. She was so kind and full of life. I just wish I could apologize for forgetting, for all these years, how special both my friends were. I should have trusted them.' She nodded at Elly's pendant. 'I'm so glad you're still wearing that. And Tash and Sierra should wear theirs too. I hope you learn from my mistakes. Your friends are more important than any treasure.'

Tash was staring at her mum as if she'd never met her before.

Sierra turned to her dad. 'I guess I'd like to stay for a while after all, if you don't mind.'

'A few minutes ago I was afraid I'd lost you.'

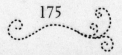

Mr Cruz's voice was very quiet. 'I have never been so scared. Please stay.' He gave her an awkward kiss on the cheek.

'I want to stay too,' Elly told Aunt Dina.

'You do surprise me.' Her aunt was smiling, but a look in her eyes told Elly that an extended lecture entitled 'Running Off on Rescue Missions Without Permission' was logged in the Official Aunt Diary.

Sierra fished her bracelet from her waterproof. Tash dug her pin out of her soaked jeans pocket. They put them on, linked arms with Elly, and began to walk home. Mojo scampered ahead. Elly thought he looked rather pleased with himself.

'What shall we do tomorrow?' Tash asked. 'Sailing, surfing or exploring?'

'Art lessons!' Aunt Dina's voice chased them across Mirror Cove. 'I'm not letting the three of you out of my sight for at least a day! Art lessons and peach muffins! And tea cosies don't crochet themselves, you know.'

'Muffins? Out-and-out bribery.' Sierra cocked her head to consider. 'And it's working.'

'Half a day, maybe,' Tash said. 'Then we hit the surf.'

It was going to be a long and glorious summer. Elly turned and grinned at her aunt. 'Forget about the tea cosies and we've got a deal!'

**Turn over for a sneaky peek
at the next book in
The Flip-Flop Club series**

Turn over for a sneaky peek
at the next book in
The Flip-Flop Club series

Chapter 1

'It's not worth being famous if I have to get up at five a.m.,' Sierra grumbled, yawning and shivering in the chilly dawn air. 'And I'm not even sure I want my picture in the paper looking like this!' She tugged at her too-short, Tash-sized wetsuit, staring mournfully at her feet which were very un-Sierra-like in neoprene wetshoes instead of sparkly flip-flops.

Elly smiled in sympathy but grabbed her friend's hand and pulled her after Tash. 'Come on! She's leaving us behind!'

'You have to get up early to go whale-spotting.'

Tash strode ahead of them across the beach. 'I hope the rumours are true and that there really are Northern Bottlenose whales headed our way. They're rare this far south.'

'We just *have* to win *The Sunday Island News* contest and be the first to get a photograph of them,' Elly said.

'I'll do my best!' Tash patted the waterproof camera she wore around her neck.

'It's the photo of *us* I'm worried about!' Sierra muttered.

'Don't worry,' Tash said, whirling round to grin at Sierra. 'The news crew will have a hair stylist, and someone to do manicures.'

'Really?' Sierra's face lit up, then fell. 'Oh, I nearly fell for that. OK. We find the whales first, then I stress. Deal?'

'Deal!' Elly was suddenly so excited she felt she might explode. She let go of Sierra and leapt over a mound  of seaweed, whooping in delight. The wetsuit Tash had lent her made her feel like a real sailor. And today they were going to leave the harbour for open sea. Her tummy went all butterflies and squirms at the thought.

The morning sun hung just above the eastern sea and the beach of Sunday Island's main harbour was washed clean by the tide. Sailing boat rigging clinked in the steady off-shore breeze and seagulls screamed overhead. Other than a small fleet of dinghies dozing on the sand and a flock of wading birds dodging the waves, the girls were alone. Mojo, Tash's border terrier, spotted the birds and gave chase, bounding across the damp sand. With a clattering of wings, the birds took to the air before wheeling off to find a dog-free stretch of sand.

Elly slid to a stop, watching the birds.

Everything smelt of sea and freshness. What a morning for an adventure!

'I've seen Minke whales before, but never a Northern Bottlenose. It would be so great if we spotted one.' Tash's voice was wistful. Elly knew that Tash had photographs of whales and dolphins stuck all over the walls of her bedroom and tree house. Today was obviously pretty special for her.

Tash whistled Mojo to heel as they reached her blue Wayfarer dinghy, named the *Mojo* after him. He trotted over to them, panting and wagging his tail. 'Good dog!' Tash gave him a pat, then slid off her backpack and stowed it in the boat. 'OK, give me your stuff too.' She turned around and her eyes widened in disbelief at the sight of Sierra's enormous purple handbag, which her friend was wearing slung over her wetsuit. 'Why on earth did you bring *that*?' Tash began to splutter with laughter.

'I've got lots of really important stuff in here,' Sierra said, hugging her handbag close. 'I need to keep it with me.'

Elly shrugged her backpack off her shoulders. In her rush to make the dawn rendezvous she hadn't bothered to fasten it properly. Now, as she struggled to close the zip, the backpack slipped from her fingers. It hit the ground, dumping all her stuff onto the sand.

'Watch out, you'll get sand in our sandwiches!' Sierra knelt to help Elly repack. She plucked a book from the sand. 'What's this?'

'A book?' Tash exclaimed. 'The *Mojo* isn't exactly a cruise liner, you know. No deckchairs and skittles.'

'No fancy restaurant with five course meals

185

either.' Sierra sighed wistfully, rubbing her tummy. 'I'm starving!'

'You should have had breakfast,' Tash said.

'I did! Sea air makes me hungry.'

'Everything makes you hungry.' Elly shook her head in mock despair. 'You're going to have to become a chef.'

'Great idea.' Sierra's eyes sparkled. 'With my own TV show.' She waved to an invisible camera, and then handed the book to Elly.

'I brought the book to show you both,' Elly said. 'Aunt Dina gave it to me last night. It's an Edith Builtmore sailing adventure. My aunt says Edith Builtmore used to live on Sunday Island.'

'Which one is it?' Tash reached for the book. *'The Secret of Harebell Island*. That's one of my favourites. I have every book Edith Builtmore ever wrote. She was into marine  ecology long before it was trendy, and she was a world class sailor.' Tash paused. 'Did you know she was returning to Sunday Island after sailing the Atlantic single-handed when she disappeared? They never found any trace of her or her yacht.'

'That's sad.' Sierra shivered. 'And mysterious. I wonder what happened to her? Maybe she's still stranded on a desert island somewhere.'

'She'd be super-old by now,' Elly said. She tried to imagine being out in the open sea all alone. Edith Builtmore must have been very brave.

Tash turned the book over and studied the author's photograph. 'Someday I'm going to sail around the world single-handed.'

'Now I know you're crazy.' Sierra made a face. 'Days without anyone to talk to? Or a hot shower? Urgh!' She took the book from Tash and flipped through it. 'This looks good.

Can I read it when you're finished, Elly?'

'Sure,' Elly said. 'It's about three girls. I just wondered . . . is it too weird or could she have been writing about our mums? They would have been on the island about the same time she was. It would be so cool if they inspired one of Edith Builtmore's books.'

Elly thought about the photograph the three of them had found in Tash's attic, the one of their mothers as girls on Sunday Island. They had been best friends too. She had framed a copy of the photo and hung it on the wall of her bedroom in Aunt Dina's cottage. It was her second most precious possession.

She reached up to touch the chain of the silver charm she always wore around her neck. She'd tucked it inside her wetsuit to keep it safe. Each of them had inherited a friendship charm from their mothers, and had sworn never to take them off. Tash's charm was pinned to her wetsuit and Sierra's dangled among the clutter of bangles on her wrist.

Sierra's eyes were bright with excitement. 'I bet you're right. Our mums are secretly famous.'

'And if we want to be famous too, we need to get going before someone else beats us to those whales!' Tash interrupted. 'We need to be the first to spot them, remember?'

Elly slid the book into her backpack. She fastened the zip securely before handing the pack to Tash, who stored it in one of the waterproof cargo bags tucked against the side of the boat.

Then she tugged out some life jackets and handed them round. 'Essential equipment, guys.'

'But this thing is . . . *orange!*' Sierra's eyes

widened in horror. 'Orange makes my skin look green.'

'Sorry, Sierra.' Tash was doing her best not to smile. 'Even Mojo has to wear one.' She knelt to slip a bright orange dog-shaped life jacket onto the border terrier's back, fastening it with chest and belly straps. Mojo whined but stood patiently, obviously used to the routine. 'Safety before fashion.'

'I guess,' Sierra said sadly as she pulled on the life jacket. 'Oh well, at least my armbands are pink.'

'Armbands?' Elly said, before she could stop herself. Tash was staring, open-mouthed.

'Absolutely,' Sierra said firmly. 'Essential for the ocean-going lady of fashion.' She tugged some bits of plastic from a mesh pocket on her wetsuit and proceeded to blow up a pair of neon-pink armbands, which she slid up her

arms. When she had finished, she struck a muscle-pose. 'What d'ya think?'

Elly began to splutter. Tash was already whooping in hysterics.

Sierra grinned at them. 'OK, so I'm a scaredy-cat, but the armbands make me happier about going out to sea in this teensy little boat.'

'Totally you, Sierra.' Elly decided this wasn't the time to mention that neon-pink armbands and a fluorescent orange vest were an eye-watering combination.

'Come on,' said Tash, when she got her breath back. 'Let's get the *Mojo* launched before the rest of the island wakes up and beats us to the whales.'

Mojo lifted his ears at the sound of his name and barked.

'All dogs on board!' Tash scooped the border terrier into the bottom of the boat, where he

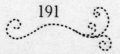

sat perfectly still, like the trained sailor he was. Tash lifted the front bar of the two-wheeled trailer and began to back her boat towards the sea. As soon as she was knee-deep in the water, Tash unhooked the ties and floated the boat off the trailer. She steadied the dinghy in the bobbing waves as Elly and Sierra towed the trailer back up onto the beach. Then they splashed into the sea and held the boat while Tash hopped in. She stood in the centre of the boat, untying the ropes securing the sail. She took her place at the tiller. 'Come aboard and raise the mainsail, First Officer Elly!'

Sierra kept the dinghy steady as Elly hitched herself over the side of the boat and found the rope used to raise and lower the dinghy's large triangular sail. She pulled it in hand over hand, as Tash had taught her. The mainsail slowly unfurled and began to flap

in the breeze. When
it reached the top of
the mast, Elly secured
the rope and settled
back, her heart thudding with
excitement as the sail filled and the boat
started to slide through the water.

Sierra quickly hauled herself over the side.
'You can't leave without me!'

'Raise the jib, Second Officer Sierra!' Tash
called.

Sierra made quick work of raising the
tiny jib sail, which was soon ballooning out
in front of the mast. The dinghy picked up
speed, riding as gently as a rocking horse over
the bouncing waves. The *Mojo* steered crisply
away from shore.

Elly sat back on the wooden ledge that served
as a seat. Sierra sat opposite her, clutching
the sides of the boat with both hands. Tash
guided them towards choppier water at the

head of the harbour. The boat cut through the waves, bobbing up and down, as the *Mojo* headed out into open sea. The whale-sighting expedition had begun!

A Note from the Author

I grew up in Missouri, as far from the sea as it is possible to be in the United States. The long, hot summer holidays were spent swimming and canoeing on the lakes and rivers. My sisters, cousins and I watched crayfish wriggle along the creekbeds, waded in the streams and had our toes nibbled by swarms of minnows darting through the clear limestone waters. We snorkelled in the lakes and pretended we were diving among coral reefs and rainbow-coloured fish instead of Missouri mud and whiskery catfish. Childhood summers were full of barbecues, homemade ice cream, watermelon

and twilight evenings spent catching fireflies in order to let them go and watch them spiral into the air like sparks from a bonfire.

All the time I was growing

up, I longed to see the ocean and finally did on a school trip when I was the same age as Elly, Tash and Sierra. I'll never forget swimming with my friends in the sea for the first time.

Now I live in England with my family, and every summer, we spend as much time as we can on an island. My love for British islands is a big part of the joy of writing the Flip-Flop books. On my first trip to the Isles of Scilly I fell in love with the small whiskery dog of one of the boatmen: a proper seadog who trotted around the boat taking us between the islands with a cocky assurance that charmed me. I've been waiting ever since for a chance to write about Mojo! As I write, I'm taken back to some of my favourite places on earth, places very much like Sunday Island.

Ellen Richardson x

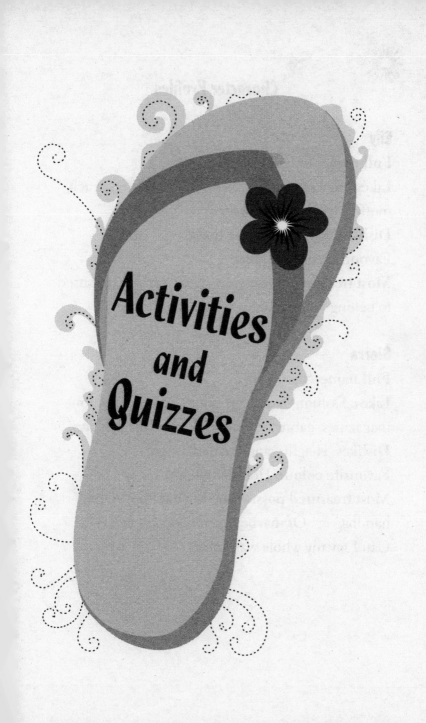

Activities
and
Quizzes

Character Profiles

Elly

Full name: Eleanor Porter

Likes: Adventures! TV shows, films, acting, peach muffins (yum!), and hugs

Dislikes: Having nothing to do

Favourite colour: Green

Most treasured possession: The necklace that used to belong to my mum.

Sierra

Full name: Sierra Cruz

Likes: Fashion, handbags, shoes, bangles, fashion magazines, eating, swimming, and crazy dancing

Dislikes: Heights, and the dark (urgh!)

Favourite colour: Hot hot hot pink

Most treasured possession: My flip-flops! Or my handbag . . . Or maybe my pink denim jacket . . . ? Can I say my whole wardrobe?

Tash

Full name: Natasha Blake-Reynolds

Likes: Sailing, surfing, my dog Mojo, being outdoors, seals, sea birds, dolphins, whales, and my tree house

Dislikes: Trying to be as clean as my mum would like

Favourite colour: Purple

Most treasured possession: Mojo—the dog and the boat!

Mojo

Full name: Mojo cute-cuddly-and-cool Blake-Reynolds

Likes: Tash, Elly, Sierra, cuddles, treats, walks, digging, and doughnuts (drool!)

Dislikes: Sitting still

You

Full name: ------------------------------------

Likes: ------------------------------------

Dislikes: ------------------------------------

Favourite colour: ------------------------------------

Most treasured possession: ------------------------------------

Are you like Elly, Tash, or Sierra?
Tick the statements that most remind you of you.

I love painting my nails crazy colours!

Sometimes, I'd rather be with animals than with people

Trainers are the best kind of shoes (after flip-flops of course!)

Hugs always help

I am always hungry!

I love the sea

TV is an essential part of life!

Chocolate ice-cream is the only ice-cream worth eating!

The bigger your handbag – the better!

There are too many yummy flavours of ice-cream to have a favourite!

I have a fiery temper

A girl can never have too many pairs of shoes

I'm very determined

I'd rather be outside than inside

I'd rather be shopping than rock-climbing

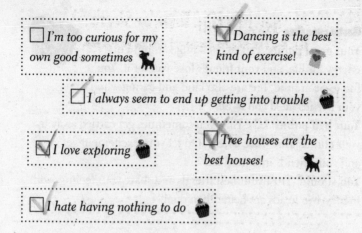

☐ I'm too curious for my own good sometimes 🐕

☑ Dancing is the best kind of exercise! 👕

☑ I always seem to end up getting into trouble 🧁

☑ I love exploring 🧁

☑ Tree houses are the best houses! 🐕

☑ I hate having nothing to do 🧁

Count up your scores...

🧁 = 4

🐕 = 43

👕 = 5

Turn over to find out which member of The Flip-Flop Club you're most like...

Answers

Mostly cupcakes: You're like Elly

Your good points: You've got a huge amount of energy for life, and your friends love you for it. You're fun to be around, but are also kind and caring when your friends need you to be.

Your bad points: Like Elly, you sometimes get carried away by your enthusiasm! Take care not to let your excitement get you and your friends into trouble.

You should: Trust your best friends and share your feelings with them—two heads are better than one!

Mostly Mojos: You're like Tash

Your good points: You're independent and adventurous like Tash, and know how to make anything more fun for you and your friends!

Your bad points: Like Tash, you can be a bit shy around new people. Take a deep breath and say what you've got to say—your friends will back you up!

You should: Be proud of yourself for being the great person you are!

Mostly T-shirts: You're like Sierra

Your good points: You're fun and passionate, and very loyal to your friends.

Your bad points: Like Sierra, you have a fiery temper! Walk away from heated situations before you lose it, and try again when you've calmed down.

You should: Not expect everyone to be as great a friend as you! Sometimes people are busy, or get distracted by other things. Remember that everyone has their own strengths!

Word Search

B	R	D	J	M	U	F	F	I	N	J	A
P	H	E	L	Q	H	S	A	T	C	R	Z
E	U	O	M	A	J	N	W	R	R	H	Y
L	R	T	L	M	O	J	O	E	Z	B	S
L	G	U	J	I	U	Q	I	E	Y	C	P
Y	R	A	S	C	D	S	K	H	R	H	O
K	B	Q	O	A	M	A	F	O	V	A	L
H	M	Y	S	T	E	R	Y	U	J	R	F
C	S	A	J	H	I	R	F	S	K	M	P
A	W	O	Z	M	D	U	T	E	A	Z	I
E	F	R	I	E	N	D	S	H	I	P	L
B	G	A	B	D	N	A	H	K	B	W	F

ELLY	MOJO	HOLIDAYS
TASH	MYSTERY	BEACH
SIERRA	MAZE	MUFFIN
CHARM	FLIP FLOPS	HANDBAG
SUMMER	TREE HOUSE	
FRIENDSHIP	TREASURE	

Customize Your Own Flip-Flops!

Get the craft box out and decorate a pair of flip-flops!

This is a fun way to have some really gorgeous and unique flip-flops that everyone will want!

Things you'll need: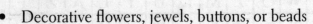

- 1 pair of flip-flops
- Ribbon
- Superglue
- Scissors
- Decorative flowers, jewels, buttons, or beads

Step 1:

Start with the ribbon. Wrap a length of it around the strap of each flip-flop, using a small drop of glue to hold the ends in place. You could use several different colours of ribbon to make your feet really stand out! Or you might be able to find ribbon with beads attached to add some Sierra glamour!

Step 2:

Use glue to add embellishments such as flowers and buttons to the straps, and to the edges of the flip-flops. Some craft shops sell stick-on jewels and charms which are perfect for this.

Step 3:

Give your flip-flops time to dry thoroughly before wearing them—or you might end up with them glued to your feet!

Top Tips

- Put some newspaper down to work on to protect tables and floors from any spilt glue!
- Cutting the ribbon diagonally will prevent it from fraying.
- For a super-quick fashion fix, try tying some wide ribbon in a pretty bow on your flip-flop straps.
- Look out for other fun things to customize your flip-flops with: glitter, colourful fur, scrabble letters, coins, goggle-eyes, and pretty material all work well!

Charmed Summer Scavenger Hunt

Answer the questions below and unscramble the highlighted letters to find the code which unlocks a secret section of *The Flip-Flop Club* website:

www.the-flip-flop-club.com

1. Where do Elly and Sierra meet for the first time?
(Hint: p. 23)

__ ▨ __ ▨ __ __ __ __ __

2. What does Aunt Dina like to crochet?
(Hint: p. 1 and p. 185)

__ ▨ __ / __ __ __ __ __ __

3. What is Elly's mum's first name? (Hint: p. 18)

__ __ ▨ __ __ __ __ ▨ __

4. What colour is Sierra's handbag? (Hint: p. 28)

__ __ ▨ __ __ __ __

5. Where do the girls have their midnight feast?
(Hint: p. 38)

__ __ __ ▨ __ __ __ __ __

6. What is the name of Tash's dog? (Hint: p. 35)

_ ▓ _ _

7. What do the islanders call Sunday Island?
(Hint: p. 38 and 39)

_ _ _ _ _ _ _ / ▓ _ _ _ _ _ ▓

8. What present does Sierra give Tash and Elly?
(Hint: p. 99 and p. 101)

▓ _ _ _ _ / ▓ _ _ _ ▓

9. What have the girls' mums buried in the hidden cave?
(Hint: p. 143)

_ _ _ _ _ / _ _ _ _ _ _ _ ▓

SECRET CODE:
Unscramble the highlighted letters and fill in the blanks below:
F _ _ _ _ _ _ / F_ _ / E _ _ _

Create Your Own Time Capsule!

You can make your own time capsule, just like the one Elly, Tash, and Sierra find in the cave! You could create one by yourself, for your future self to open in five or ten years' time. Or you could team up with your best friends, like Elly's, Tash's, and Sierra's mums did. A time capsule can be as simple as a shoebox full of items, put on a shelf or stashed away in a cupboard and forgotten about until a later date.

Questions to ask yourself before you start:

- Would you like to open the time capsule yourself?
- Would you like the time capsule to last long into the future and be found by someone you never knew?
- Where will you store your time capsule? Burying it may not be the best choice as it may get forgotten, lost, or damaged by animals or wet weather.
- What container will you use? This might depend on how much you want to put in, and where you're planning on putting it. If you're going to store it inside, a shoebox or biscuit tin are good ideas. If you plan to place the time capsule outdoors or bury the time capsule, you'll need a waterproof container.

Now, collect the things to go in your time capsule.

Who will open your time capsule, and what would you like to tell them? Have fun with this step! Choose things that are special to you now—but not things that you'll miss, or that don't belong to you. You could choose anything, but here are a few ideas:

- Photographs
- Old diaries
- Letters
- Newspapers or magazines
- Coins

You could also write a letter about what your life is like. Write about your favourite food, your favourite music, your pets, what you like to wear and what you like to do, your dreams and ambitions for the future, and who your best friends are. Imagine reading it in ten years' time!

Do something to remind yourself or others where the time capsule is and the date you intend it to be opened.

If you have a calendar, you could write at the end of it each year when your time capsule should be opened. Place a marker if you have hidden or buried the time capsule, indicating where it can be found. If you're going to open your time capsule, you could choose a special opening date, such as your 16th birthday. Do you think much will have changed?

Aunt Dina's Peach and Cinnamon Muffins

You will need an adult helper when it comes to using the oven

Ingredients

- 1 egg
- 120ml milk
- 4 tbsp oil
- 200g plain flour
- 100g caster sugar
- 2 tbsp baking powder
- 3 ripe peaches chopped into 1cm cubes
- a large pinch of cinnamon

Method

1. Preheat the oven to 180°C/350°F/Gas Mark 4 and line a muffin tray with paper cases.
2. Beat the egg, then stir in the milk and oil.
3. Sift the flour into a large bowl. Add the sugar and baking powder.
4. Add the egg mix to the flour mix and stir gently.
5. Fold in the chopped peach and the cinnamon. Don't worry if the mix isn't smooth.
6. Spoon the mixture into the paper cases in the tray.
7. Bake on the middle shelf of the oven for 20-25 minutes.
8. Transfer the cooked muffins to a wire rack to cool.

Try

Get fruity : Try apples, apricots, or plums instead of peaches.

Aunt Dina's Favourite Fairy Cakes

You will need an adult helper when it comes to using the oven

Ingredients

For the cakes

- 2 eggs
- 100g caster sugar
- 100g self-raising flour
- 100g butter (softened)

For the chocolate buttercream icing

- 50g butter (softened)
- 100g sifted icing sugar
- 50g cocoa powder, sifted
- 1-2 tbsp milk

To decorate

- white chocolate buttons

Method

1. Preheat the oven to 180°C/350°F/Gas Mark 4 and line a fairy cake tin with paper cases.
2. Cream the butter and sugar together in a bowl until light and fluffy.
3. Beat in the eggs one at a time, adding a little flour with each.
4. Gently mix in the rest of the flour.
5. Half fill the paper cases with the mixture.
6. Bake the cakes for 15-20 minutes, or until golden-brown on top and a skewer inserted into one of the cakes comes out clean. Set aside to cool for 10 minutes on a wire rack before removing from the tin.
7. To make the buttercream, beat the butter in a large bowl until soft. Add half of the icing sugar and beat until smooth.
8. Add the remaining icing sugar, cocoa powder, and one tablespoon of the milk, and beat until creamy. Beat in more milk if necessary to loosen the icing.
9. Once the cakes are cool, spread the buttercream icing on top of the cakes.
10. Decorate the cakes with the chocolate buttons, and hey presto:

You've got scrumptious fairy cakes to share with your friends!

Want to join

The FLiP FLOP Club?

Find out more about Elly, Tash, Sierra, and Mojo on The Flip-Flop Club website!

www.the-flip-flop-club.com

Log on for quizzes and activities, as well as exclusive competitions and giveaways!